An Inconvenient Love

Alexia Adams

Copyright

An Inconvenient Love
By Alexia Adams
Copyright 2014 by Alexia Adams

Published by:
Alexia Adams
Suite 377
255 Newport Drive
Port Moody, BC V3H 5H1
Canada

Contact: Alexia@alexia-adams.com
www.alexia-adams.com

Edited by Julie Sturgeon
Cover design by Katie Kenyhercz

Ebook ISBN 978-1-9991756-3-4
Print ISBN 978-1-9991756-7-2

First Edition June 2014
Second Edition November 2019
First Print Edition October 2020

Product of Canada

Dedication

This book is dedicated to my sister-in-law Samantha and my critique partner Ellie Darkins, neither of whom would let me give up on Luca and Sophia.

Acknowledgments

I'd like to acknowledge the huge contribution of my editor, Julie Sturgeon. You saw the potential in this book and guided me to finding the true story of Luca and Sophia's love. Your sense of humor and awesome suggestions made the editing process much less painful than it would otherwise have been. You are amazing.

And, of course, I have to acknowledge the support of my long-suffering family. I promise I'll clean the house … as soon as the next book is finished.

Chapter One

F2. Deal again.

The workday was endless when your biggest decision was FreeCell or solitaire. Today solitaire was the game of choice, and Sophia was already $830 down. Damn Vegas scoring. At least she didn't have to worry about anyone knocking at her door to collect that debt.

The front doorbell buzzed, and she switched the display on her monitor from the game to webcam. Metal chair legs scraping against the wood floor indicated that the elderly porter had been awakened from his nap and was on the way to answer the summons.

Look up, look up, she mentally willed the man standing at the door, waiting to be let in. Her telepathy not working, she tried adjusting the camera angle to get a better view, but all she could see was the top of his head. Dark hair, that was all. Useless angle, useless camera.

Not that she held out much hope that he would be worth looking at. The managing partner had mentioned as he passed her desk this morning that an important Italian property developer was coming to meet with him. An image of a short, middle-aged man with a Donald Trump hairstyle came to her mind, and she suppressed a giggle.

The visitor eventually arrived at the reception area.

A Georgian house didn't lend itself to the most efficient layout for an office. Trying to at least appear busy, Sophia pretended to save a document before turning to greet the man. She looked up, way up. Okay, so not short. And his black, slightly curly hair was brushed back from his face and bore absolutely no resemblance to Donald Trump's. In fact, her fingers itched to run through it and release the curls further. His strong jaw and Roman nose looked like an advertisement for some amazing facial makeover. Dressed in a dark gray suit, he had an air of power. Even dressed more casually she was sure he would still have an aura of command.

This was no middle-aged specimen. The man standing before her was definitely in his prime. If he were a steer, he'd have AAA stamped on his left butt cheek, another image that left her battling the giggles. Until his dark eyes met hers, and all the air was sucked out of her lungs. He was so gorgeous, she clamped her lips together so she didn't accidently drool on her keyboard.

"Luca Castellioni to see Walter Bodman." His deep voice held only a hint of an Italian accent.

"Oh, yes, Mr. Castellioni. If you'd like to take a seat, I'll let Mr. Bodman know that you're here."

The guest smiled, as if distracted by a pleasant memory, and sat across the room in direct sight of her desk. Her suddenly nervous fingers had to twice dial the senior partner's secretary, and her voice came out all breathless when she announced the visitor.

"Mr. Bodman is just finishing up a conference call. He'll be down shortly." At least she managed to sound a little normal.

The enigmatic visitor acknowledged her statement and picked up a magazine from the table next to him. But every time she looked up, he was staring at her rather than reading. He made no effort to look away, and it was Sophia who broke the eye contact each time. She was sure he could hear her heartbeat pounding from across the room. The more she tried to ignore his presence, the more acutely she became aware of his every movement.

Walter Bodman's gruff voice booming across the room had never been so welcome. "Luca! Sorry to have kept you waiting. How wonderful to see you again. It's been what—three years?"

"Five," the Italian corrected. "You are doing well. Very nice offices…" His voice trailed away as he followed his host.

A sharp stab of pain made Sophia aware she'd been clenching her toes. She kicked off her sensible ballerina flats and dreamed for a moment of the handsome Italian massaging her feet. There was no way she was going to be able to go back to her game of solitaire now.

Her mobile phone vibrated on the desk beside her. The bank was kindly advising that her account was now down to fourteen pounds fifty pence, and still six days to payday. With the tuition due for the next term of her interior design studies, her finances wouldn't be much better even after she was paid.

She logged on to a job finder website, but there wasn't much call for a receptionist with minimal experience and no real desire to do the job. And none paid more than what she was making now. Her desk phone buzzed, and she shut down the webpage. Might as well do the job she had, rather than worry about the one she couldn't get.

An hour later Sophia was transcribing a letter one of the secretaries sent down when a shadow crossed her screen and the hair on the back of her neck stood on end. A hint of sandalwood and citrus tickled her nose. Looking up, she wasn't surprised to see the Italian businessman standing at her desk.

"I look forward to seeing you tonight, Miss Stevens."

"I … ah … I … how do you know my name?" She latched onto the first thing that came to mind while she tried to make sense of his words.

He pointed at the small plaque on her desk with her name inscribed. "Walter has invited me to the company party. I hope we will have the opportunity to talk. Until tonight…" Turning on his heel, he strode from the room.

Why would a gorgeous Italian millionaire want to talk to me? Her toes curled again.

• • •

Luca entered the marquee in St. James's Square and searched for Walter. At least that's what his brain told his eyes to look for. They decided to hunt down the blonde receptionist instead. She was beautiful. But he knew lots of beautiful women. Maybe it was the laughter in her green eyes or the way she'd tried not to notice him that intrigued him. Whatever it was, he couldn't relax until he spotted her.

She stood twenty meters away, chatting with a couple of other women, a glass of champagne in her hand. Her simple black dress was elegant and alluring, hugging her curves rather than pushing them up for all to see. His pulse quickened, as it had when he had seen her in the office. Before he could approach her, Walter's over-loud voice stopped him.

"Luca, glad you could join us. I want to introduce you to Chet Wilkins, an American business acquaintance. He's scouting new locations for his boutique hotel chain. He's looking for rural properties to turn into luxury spas where stressed executives can go to relax. But I'll let him tell you all the requirements."

Walter led him to a tall, thin man in his early sixties, standing beside a woman of similar age who was wearing too little dress and too much makeup. Luca glanced to where Sophia had been chatting, only to find she was no longer with the group of women. Forcing his mind back to business, he smiled at the American couple.

Thirty minutes later, his smile was strained and he shifted another couple centimeters away from Mrs. Leslie Wilkins. She stood so close, he was in danger of suffocating on her cloying perfume. And he was pretty damn sure it wasn't by accident she kept brushing his thigh or backside with her hand. Her husband continued to drone on about the ideal properties he was looking for, completely ignoring his wife. Walter had excused himself ten minutes ago, so it was just the three of them, penned into a corner. A waiter passed and Leslie grabbed yet another glass of champagne.

"Luca, there you are. I wondered where you'd got to." The sexy voice of Walter's receptionist halted the glass halfway to the American woman's lips. Sophia's small hand slipped into his, and he gave it a squeeze of appreciation.

He glanced down at her upturned face and had to stop himself from bending down and kissing her slightly parted lips. Sophia did weird things to his self-control. He was probably in more danger from her than Leslie Wilkins. "My apologies, *amore*. Walter introduced me to Mr. and Mrs. Wilkins, and we got so engrossed in our conversation, I lost track of time. Leslie, Chet, do you know Sophia Stevens?"

Leslie Wilkins downed half the glass of champagne in one go and turned to her husband. "I'm going to get something to eat," she said before walking away, her steps wobbly.

"Nice to see you again, Mr. Wilkins. Pardon me, I didn't mean to interrupt your conversation," Sophia added. "I'll make sure Mrs. Wilkins finds the buffet okay."

As quietly as she'd arrived, Sophia left, a light, lingering scent of fresh fruit and an odd tingle in his palm the only remnants of her appearance. Without missing a beat, Chet Wilkins continued his property wish list.

"I know of three properties that would suit your needs. When will you be in Italy?" As much as he'd love to cement a relationship with Chet, he couldn't keep his mind off Sophia. Maybe she'd been checking him out and noticed his discomfort? His breath caught in his chest. What other hidden talents did the beguiling receptionist possess?

Chet's voice interrupted his contemplations. "We'll be there in about six weeks. My wife is accompanying me."

Luca took a sip of his drink to expunge the bad taste in his mouth at the thought of more time in the company of Leslie Wilkins. "Here's my card. Call me when you firm up your plans. I believe we can enjoy a mutually beneficial business partnership."

Chet Wilkins pocketed his card and shook hands. "I look forward to working with you. Guess I'd better round up Leslie," he said, then wandered toward the bar area rather than the buffet. Apparently, the man knew exactly where he'd find his wife.

Luca scanned the crowd, ignoring the open invitation on several of the women's faces. Eventually he found Sophia, standing alone by the ice sculpture. The tiny white lights strung through the marquee danced off her golden hair, drawing him like a moth to a flame.

"Thank you," he said, resisting the urge to take her hand again, to see if the connection he'd experienced earlier had been real.

A hesitant smile played about her lips. "I wasn't rescuing you. I was saving Chet Wilkins. He was getting more embarrassed each time she touched you. Mr. Wilkins is a nice man; he's been to the office several times. I didn't like watching his wife flirt with someone in front of him."

Damn, she hadn't been checking him out. He had to force a smile. "Well, whatever your motive, I am grateful. Can I get you another drink?" He glanced down at her hand; the champagne was still at the same level it had been when he'd first seen her almost forty-five minutes ago.

"No, I'm good. Don't let me detain you. I'm sure there must be other important people here you'd like to talk with."

Was she trying to get rid of him? She'd met his gaze briefly before staring at his left shoulder. "Why do you feel you are not important?"

"I'm the receptionist." She shrugged, her gaze only flicking to his momentarily.

"Receptionists are the first introduction to a company. They are vital in portraying the correct image. You should never think less of yourself."

"It's only a job."

"Well if you could be anything you wanted, what would it be?"

"A ninja." This time her eyes did meet his and the laughter was back in their green depths.

Whether it was the audacity of her reply or her smile he wasn't sure, but he sucked in a deep breath. "An interesting career choice. Why would you like to be a ninja?"

"Black's my favorite color." Her flippant answer made him smile.

"So what is holding you back? A lack of black outfits?"

She laughed. "Ah, if only. No, the best ninja schools are in Japan, and I don't have a passport." She shrugged and looked once again over his shoulder.

"Am I keeping you from someone? Your husband or boyfriend?" He'd noticed in the office she didn't wear a ring, and there had been no photos on her desk. But that didn't mean she wasn't involved with someone. He repressed the disappointment that swept through him.

"No, I'm here alone. I only came because Mr. Bodman insisted everyone in the company attend. But I think I've stayed long enough. I see Mr. Wilkins steering his wife toward the exit, so you should be safe now."

"Safe, thanks to you. In fact your timely intervention has given me an idea. Will you meet me tomorrow? I have an opportunity I would like to discuss with you."

"You need an untrained ninja to protect you?"

"Something like that."

Sophia tilted her head to one side and stared at him. Finally she shrugged her delicate shoulders again. "I usually take a walk around St. James's Park at lunchtime. I'll be on the bridge at 12:30 if you still want to talk with me." She spoke as though she didn't really believe he would show up.

"Tomorrow at 12:30 then."

Her eyes searched his face but he kept his expression carefully neutral. If she discovered his interest, she may not come. The plan that had started when she slipped her hand into his had solidified with their brief conversation. Yes, Sophia Stevens would do very nicely.

• • •

Sophia stood on the bridge and looked out over the lake to the fountain and Buckingham Palace in the background. Spring had come early; the trees were in bloom and crocuses and daffodils soaked up the sunshine. To stop from searching for Luca, she stared at the ducks. A male mallard was enticing a female with a display of his bright plumage. She wished she were a duck. They didn't worry about paying the rent or putting their brother through college.

She should have brought some water to drink. Her mouth was so dry, she may not be able to talk. If he came. Having tossed and turned half the night, she'd finally reached the conclusion that Luca must be opening an office in London and wanted to employ her. Then she'd spent the rest of the night working out exactly how much salary she could reasonably request. If she asked for too much, he'd think her greedy. If she asked for too little, she'd be a drone for the rest of her life, never achieving her dream of her own interior design company.

The question she hadn't been able to answer was whether she could actually work for him. She'd been unable to concentrate when he sat across from her in the office. And then last night at the party she could barely meet his gaze, sure he'd be able to see through her veil of bravado to the frightened girl inside.

Lost in her problems, she didn't notice Luca approach until his arm brushed hers on the bridge rail. She took a deep, calming breath. Her mouth suddenly started to salivate, and his intoxicating aftershave lured her to lean closer. He'd come.

"I am pleased to see you again." Perhaps it was her imagination, but his accent seemed thicker today. He was immaculate, not a hair out of place, his suit undoubtedly costing more than she made all month. He was way beyond her league. What else could he want except a receptionist?

"You said you had a job opportunity to discuss with me." She moved her arm away so they no longer touched. What was he playing at? Did he think because she'd slipped her hand into his at the party that she was available for an affair? Well, if so, he'd find out soon enough she wasn't going to sleep with him just because he was rich, and powerful, and gorgeous.

"An opportunity, yes. As you know, I own a property development and restoration company in the north of Italy, based in Milan." His low voice, so close, sounded like they were sharing an illicit secret. "I am now in a position to sign some large contracts with British and American companies, like Chet Wilkins. However, my secretary, who is very good, does not speak fluent English. I cannot afford to have misunderstandings."

Excitement raced through her. It was a job offer. And from the sound of it, based in Italy. She was tired of London. Tired of working two, sometimes three, jobs just to make ends meet, never getting ahead. A move to Italy would be the change she longed for, a chance to escape the constant reminders of her horrific past. Before she could respond however, he continued.

"I need more than just an English-speaking secretary. I have reached a point in my life where all my business associates are married, and new clients are always asking about my personal life. It seems to disconcert them when I say I am unmarried, and it is becoming a hindrance to my success. Family is very important in Italy. It is seen as a sign of stability. However, my entire focus at the moment is on building my business. I do not have the time now, or in the foreseeable future, to romance a woman. Besides, a wife who loved me would expect me to be home every night and probably feel neglected with the amount of time I spend working."

Sophia struggled to keep her face neutral and not let her puzzlement show. Why was he talking about his need for a wife?

"Last night at the party you proved to me you are able to read a situation and act appropriately. I also believe you are good at your job. Walter is an astute man; he would not have kept you employed if you were not a hard worker." He leaned toward her. His voice had dropped even more, and she wondered where he was going with this so-called opportunity.

"I think, therefore, that I should align my requirements and seek an English wife. One who would be able to assist me in my business, and also provide the home life expected of a man in my position. Are you interested?" He turned to her, his eyes sweeping over her face, awaiting her response. His smile held a hint of warmth, but his eyes were guarded, as though there was something he wasn't telling. Something that prompted him to ask her, of all people.

This was it. She'd finally snapped. Her brain had

imploded from worry and boredom, and as a result she was fantasizing about marriage proposals and being swept away to live in a castle in Italy. At this point she should reach into her pocket and pull out the other glass slipper. Except the only thing in her pocket was lint. And the only romance in her life was in the books she read. Maybe Luca was the one having a meltdown? She searched his face for some sign of insanity.

He looked serious. The contents of her stomach shifted. The man had actually just proposed to her. "Mr. Castellioni, I'm sure there's a long line of suitable women who would love to marry you. We only met yesterday. And as I told you at the party, I'm just a receptionist."

"You called me Luca last evening. What has changed?"

Aside from one of them going completely insane? Him for proposing … or her for actually considering it and not walking away.

"Last night was for show, to help Mr. Wilkins. This is…"

"This is between us. I can assure you there is no other woman I would consider marrying. I realize it may seem absurd to speak of marriage when we have recently met. You said last night you were alone. Did I misunderstand? Are you in a relationship?"

"No, no, I'm not involved with anyone. But that doesn't mean I am going to run off and marry the first man who asks me," she replied. *Even if he is incredibly gorgeous. What kind of man offers marriage to a complete stranger? One who considered marriage a business arrangement, obviously. Could I do the same?*

"You do not have to give me an answer now. Have dinner with me tonight, and we can get to know each other. I would appreciate, though, if you would keep this discussion between us." He leaned forward again and there was an intensity in his dark eyes but a warmth, too, a banked passion that both unsettled and intrigued her.

Dazed, she agreed to meet him again at Quaglino's. Sophia didn't even ask how he had managed to get a table at a restaurant that was usually booked a month in advance. She was sure if he just showed up, the maître d' would lose someone else's reservation in order to accommodate him. If he expected her to bow to his every desire he was in for a shock. Sophia Stevens was no man's doormat. But she wasn't about to reject him without discovering exactly what he wanted.

And what she could get out of the deal.

Chapter Two

Luca finished his martini and put the empty glass on the bar of the West End restaurant. Sophia was forty minutes late. Perhaps he'd read the signs wrong and she wasn't coming. He was sure, though, that he'd seen a hint of curiosity in her eyes. Eyes that in the bright spring sunshine had surprised him with flecks of gold and amber amid the green.

He wouldn't blame her if she didn't show. She must think him a complete *idiota* to propose marriage after twenty-four hours. But it seemed the most logical course of action. He needed someone to proofread his English letters and a wife to deter other women.

Two weeks ago, a very important prospective client had brought his wife to their business dinner. She'd spent almost the entire evening with her hand on Luca's upper thigh under the table, despite his best efforts to remove it. He'd have shrugged it off as a bored woman looking for mischief, but she was the third wife of a business acquaintance this year who thought he was part of the package deal. Last night had been the worst because Leslie Wilkins hadn't even tried to be subtle.

He didn't do married women. Ever.

But it seemed his plan had failed before it even started. He tossed a couple of bills on the bar and was about to leave when he caught sight of Sophia standing in the doorway. His pulse quickened, but he put it down to relief that she'd showed. It had nothing to do with the way her blue dress brought out the gold in her hair, or the sway of her hips as she approached him. A little voice in his head warned that if he were a wise man, he'd get on the next plane back to Milan and forget he ever saw her. But he hadn't got where he was today by playing it safe all the time. Risk was a part of business. And this was business. The little voice laughed.

"Sorry I'm late, there was a security alert on the Tube," she greeted him. Her voice was breathy and a light flush covered her skin. Whether it was from a rush to get to the restaurant, or she experienced the same physical attraction, he wasn't sure.

"It is not a problem. Our table is ready, but if you would prefer a drink first…"

"Oh, no. I'm starved." She gave him another of her dazzling smiles.

Luca signaled to the maître d', who sat them at a prime table near the bottom of the stairs where they could see and be seen. However, he didn't take his attention from Sophia. She smelled faintly of cucumbers and melon, a refreshing change from the sickly perfume most women of his acquaintance seemed to bathe in.

She glanced around the restaurant. "I've always wanted to come here. I pass by on my way to work and wondered what it was like inside. I'm surprised you managed to get a table on a Friday night. It's packed."

"I have my ways. Shall I order champagne? Or perhaps you would like to try my country's equivalent, prosecco?"

"Not for me. Sparkling wine goes straight to my head. I'm not much of a drinker. A glass of water will do." She buried her head behind her menu, and he waited until she shut it with a decisive snap.

"Have you decided?"

"About dinner? I'll have the sea bass." She avoided his eyes again.

He wanted to ask if she'd decided about his proposal, but left the question unasked. It was unnerving how much he wanted her to say yes. For the first time he'd laid all his cards on the table and left himself open to a blunt refusal.

They should get to know each other. "Have you always lived in London?" It seemed an easy enough place to start. Except she straightened in her chair and fiddled with the cutlery next to her plate.

"Yes." She answered sharply. She took a gulp of water. "What about you? You said your company was based in Milan. Do you live in the city?"

"I have a flat in Milan where I stay if I am working late. However, I recently renovated a villa about an hour north of my office. It has extensive grounds and is on the edge of a very old village." He loved the villa, it was his dream home, visual proof that his hard work had resulted in success. Yet there was something missing—a heart and soul that couldn't be restored as easy as wood beams and plaster.

"It sounds beautiful. Is your company a family business?"

"My father was a laborer in the construction business. I worked with him during summer holidays in my teens. When he died, I started my own company. Soon I had so many contracts that I had to take on additional workers. I got my university degree by studying nights, and just completed my MBA."

"A self-made man, then. Your mother must be very happy. Do you have siblings?"

"No, I'm an only child. What about you? Do you come from a large family?"

She averted her gaze, staring over his left shoulder. "Yes, although I don't see them often. My younger brother has just finished school, and I'm trying to help him pay to go to a technical college. So why did you come to London? Was it only to meet with Mr. Bodman?"

The animation had gone from her eyes at the mention of her family, so he followed her lead in changing the topic of conversation. He sensed there was more to her quick change of subject, but for his present purposes, it would be easier to convince her to come to Italy if she weren't attached to her family in the UK.

The server was clearing their dinner plates when there was a commotion at the top of the stairs. Bright flashes of light were accompanied by calls of "Kate, Kate, look this way," drowning out the buzz of background conversations. Sophia swiveled to see what was happening and sucked in a loud breath as a woman in a short metallic dress and high heels descended.

"Excuse me," Sophia said before thrusting her chair back and hurrying from the table.

Luca half stood, not sure whether to follow her or wait for her return. She'd turned white and knocked over her water glass as she'd fled. The waiter mopped up the spill and quickly changed the linens on the table. By the time Sophia returned, all traces of her rushed departure had disappeared. Except she was still unnaturally pale and her eyes darted around the restaurant as if mapping out all the escape routes.

"I'm so sorry, Luca. But I have to leave. Thank you for a lovely dinner. I'll understand if you don't want to see me again." There was a nervous note to her voice, and she sat on the edge of her seat.

"Sophia, what is wrong? Are you ill?"

"No. It's … I don't want to be in the same room as that woman."

"What woman?" He glanced around.

"The one who arrived a few minutes ago with the photographers in tow."

"You know her?"

"Yes."

He waited for her to continue, but she didn't. "And?"

"And it's not something I wish to discuss. She is part of my past, and I have no desire to revisit it." Her voice was rough and her eyes icy.

He studied her face. There was much more to this woman than surface beauty. "I do want to see you again. Here is my business card. Call me on my mobile and we can meet again tomorrow. Perhaps spend the day together?" As he passed her his card he held her hand for a moment, shocked to find it so cold. Another shiver wracked her body, but he suspected it was from repressing her emotions rather than any awareness of his touch.

"I'm working tomorrow. The best I can do is meet you for dinner again."

"Then dinner it is," he replied.

She nodded, then grabbed her bag and scrambled up the stairs, not once looking back.

Even the little voice in his head was silent for once.

• • •

Saturday dawned gray and wet. Sophia woke up lethargic. She'd had a second sleepless night, going over the previous day in her mind. She wouldn't be surprised if Luca changed his mind about marrying her after her bizarre departure. For a few hours yesterday, she'd actually believed she was going to escape her past. Then it had come waltzing down the stairs with the paparazzi in the background.

Might as well get the rejection over with. She pulled out Luca's business card and sent him a text. That way he wouldn't have to disguise the relief in his voice when he would undoubtedly tell her he'd been called back to Italy before their meeting this evening.

Her phone binged almost immediately. A ripple of surprise flowed through her as she read his reply. He still wanted to see her and asked her to choose a restaurant where they could meet. With a smile, she texted back the address for the Thai restaurant down the street. He might as well discover now she wasn't a fine dining kind of woman. On the rare occasions she did eat out, it was cheap and cheerful. No pretension. If that didn't put him off, then maybe she'd consider his proposal. Best of all, there was no chance Kathy Summers, or Kate as she called herself now, would set one ridiculously shod foot in the door.

But first, she still had to get through today. She put on her uniform and trudged the ten blocks to the supermarket where she worked as a cashier on weekends and some evenings. She hated the job, but it helped pay the rent and kept her fed. Helping her brother through college and trying to earn her own degree in interior design had decimated her paltry savings. She was back to square one, living paycheck to paycheck. Maybe that was why she was even considering Luca's offer; it would solve all her financial worries. *Does it count as gold digging if I never actually picked up the shovel?*

Toward the end of her shift, a young mother with a baby and a toddler stood patiently in her check-out queue. The little girl, about three years old, held a huge red apple in both hands and looked up hopefully at her mother. Sophia rang through the meagre groceries: three tins of no-name brand baked beans, the cheapest loaf of bread the store sold, and some sausages with a "sell by today" clearance sticker.

"That's a lovely apple. Can I weigh it?"

Sophia put her hand out and the little girl passed the fruit as if handing her a precious possession.

"Wow, it's huge. Are you going to eat it all yourself?"

The little girl shook her head, her blonde curls bouncing about her face. "I'm gonna share it with Mummy. Georgie can't have any 'cause he doesn't have any teeth."

"I'm sure he won't mind." Sophia turned to the young mother. "Two pounds and eighty-three pence, please." She saw the mother close her eyes for a moment, then look at her daughter and shake her head. The mother picked up the apple and handed it back to Sophia before passing over the two pounds and fifty pence she'd been clutching in her fist. The child's chin dropped to her chest, but she didn't utter a word.

"Please, allow me," Sophia said softly, adding the apple to the mother's shopping bag. She'd put the extra coins in the till from her own purse. The little girl's face lit up when she saw the apple go in the grocery bag. Sophia wiped a small tear from her eye as the family left the store.

Exhausted at 6:00 p.m., she returned home, wanting only to cook a jacket potato, curl up on her chair, and read the Penny Vincenzi book she'd taken out of the library. The incident with the mother and two children had disturbed her, bringing back memories of her own childhood. The nights she'd gone to bed hungry. The embarrassment of standing in line for the free breakfast at school, while her classmates who ate at home stared at her through the window. And the teasing from her fellow students about her second-hand uniforms. She couldn't bear to put her future children through that.

It wasn't as if she were holding out for love. Her parents had been in love when they married and lived a miserable existence afterward. In her experience, marrying for love didn't always equal happiness. But she also didn't want to end up like her aunt, alone with no family, despising everyone else's relationships, secretly wishing she had someone to call her own.

Heading out the door again twenty minutes later, she felt like she was approaching a precipice. Whether she'd fall in, or make it safely across, was anybody's guess.

• • •

Sophia sat against the back wall of the Thai restaurant, her eyes trained on the door. She'd deliberately come early, wanting to see Luca's face when he arrived. If he turned up his nose at the quaint, family-run restaurant, then she'd know she couldn't marry him. There was no way she could live with a snob. It was bad enough when she had to deal with them at work.

While she waited, she inhaled the smell of lemongrass and curry—the scent of adventure. For a girl who'd never travelled more than twenty miles from where she was born, eating ethnic food was as close to a foreign holiday as she'd ever got. If she married Luca, though …

As if conjured by her thoughts, Luca strode through the door. He'd replaced the expensive suit with a pair of chocolate brown trousers and a cream button down shirt. But the change of attire hadn't diminished the sense of power he still exuded. He glanced around the tiny space, no hint of derision or condescension in his expression. When he spotted her, a smile lit his face and he strode toward her. An answering smile lifted her lips.

The hostess rushed over and handed him a plastic-coated menu which had seen better days. Despite its slightly sticky nature, he held it firmly, perusing the items as carefully as he had last night at the posh restaurant.

They ordered a selection of dishes to share and he regaled her with stories of life in Italy as they ate. Luca was attentive, ignoring his phone she could hear buzzing in his pocket from time to time. When the flustered waitress nearly dropped his plate, he simply smiled and whispered words of encouragement, wiping a splash of curry sauce from his sleeve without a second glance at the stain it had left.

It wasn't until dessert that he once again broached the subject of marriage. He leaned back and put his arm across the chair next to him. The casual pose belied the intensity in his eyes.

"I like you, Sophia. I enjoy spending time with you. I believe we could have a successful marriage. I will state up front that I do want children, although I am willing to wait a few years if that suits you better. I see this as a lifelong partnership. My parents' marriage was based on respect and agreeable companionship, and they were together for twenty years until my father died."

Her brain froze at the mention of children. She, too, wanted a family, but she hadn't stopped to consider their actual creation. The heat of Luca's gaze set off an avalanche of sensations along her skin, a tingling so physical she ran her hands up and down her arms. But having sex with someone would mean they'd discover her scars, which would lead to questions. Questions she never wanted to answer but knew she'd have to … one day.

"Couldn't I just come and work for you first? Then once we know each other better, we could get married." Even her own ears could hear the crumbling resistance in her words.

Luca leaned forward and took her hand in his, sending her pulse rate into the triple digits. "That would not be appropriate. My peers may question my integrity if I were seen dating one of my employees. And my villa is in a very small village; old-fashioned ideas still prevail. For you to live with me without being married would be frowned on. My reputation, personally and in business, is very important to me. To continue our relationship here is also not possible. I do not have the time to fly back to London every weekend."

She stared at him, mesmerized by the cadence of his voice. It all sounded so … reasonable. Luca's thumb was brushing rhythmic patterns across the back of her hand, and she had to concentrate to understand his next words.

"As my wife you will have a generous monthly allowance, in addition to credit cards and access to store accounts for any clothes, shoes, or other items you may wish to purchase. You could continue your education, get a degree in something that interests you. I am not sure there are any ninja schools in Milan, but you can check."

She laughed, surprised he'd remembered her outrageous statement at the party. "I think I'll leave ninja-ing for my next life. What do you get out of this deal?"

"All I ask is that you proofread a few letters, attend

some business functions with me from time to time, and care for our future family."

She tucked an errant strand of hair behind her ear and swallowed. His gentle caress on her hand was wreaking havoc with her normally rational thought patterns. He sounded so business-like, outlining a proposed merger of their lives, and all she could think about was the merger of their bodies. She looked down at their entwined hands and made one last attempt to match his dispassionate tone.

"I would still like to help my brother financially until he starts work full-time. May I use some of the allowance for that?"

"Of course, you can spend it on whatever you wish. If you need more, let me know. There does not seem to be anything else holding you here, so what do you say?" The words were spoken casually, but once again his accent had become more pronounced. She searched his eyes. They met her gaze with a warmth that belied the relaxed manner of his tone.

"Yes, I'll marry you and come to Italy," she said. This was her best chance to make something of herself. Complete her education, learn a new language, have a family without worrying about where the next meal was coming from. Maybe even start her own business. She'd finally be living and not merely existing. A shiver of excitement, not trepidation, raced through her.

"Excellent, I will make the arrangements. Do you truly not have a passport?" A full smile lit up his face, and Sophia wondered at the transformation. Could he have really been anxious that she would refuse him?

"No, I've never had the opportunity to travel out of the country."

"You will need to get one as soon as possible. On Monday I will have been in London for seven days, so I will meet the residency requirement and we can give notice at the register office. Then we can be wed a couple of weeks after that," he said. He had done his homework. "I know you said you don't see your family often. Perhaps I could meet your parents tomorrow?" His tone was calm, but she sensed his curiosity.

"No," she blurted out. She pulled her hand away from his and sat back in her chair, folding her arms across her chest. "Um, I don't think I'll inform my parents of our arrangement just yet. I'll tell my younger brother, James, that I have taken a job in Italy. Besides, tomorrow I'm working again. So I don't have time to see them anyway."

Luca seemed taken aback but after a moment replied, "As you wish. Do you have any other questions?"

"Not that I can think of at the moment. I am sure something will come to mind later." *Like what on earth am I thinking, marrying a complete stranger? And is this total or only partial insanity?*

Fifteen minutes later they stepped out of the restaurant into the cool West London night. The Styrofoam containers made an odd squeaking sound in the plastic bag Luca held. There had been a few leftovers from their dinner, but she hadn't wanted to appear low-class by requesting to take them home. She was pretty sure Luca's normal dates didn't ask for doggy bags. And then out of the blue, Luca ordered take-away as they finished their meal.

It turned out the extra food was for the homeless guy who lived on the street near his hotel. Luca hadn't wanted to give him money, in case he used it for drugs or alcohol, but a good meal was usually appreciated. She'd searched his face. Did he know she'd been homeless once? Was he trying to impress her with his generosity? Was it all a show?

For a minute she'd considered telling him about her past. But what if he changed his mind and she lost her chance? Her throat ached and she remained silent.

Two men stumbled out of the pub next to the restaurant and almost crashed into her. Luca quickly stepped in front, his hand reaching for hers and pulling her against his back. He took up a protective stance in front of her until the men staggered down the road, shouting obscenities to no one in particular.

"I'll walk you home," he said.

"It's not necessary, Luca. It's only a couple of blocks from here." He didn't argue. Simply raised his eyebrow and waited for her to lead the way. "Really, I've lived here for a long time. It's pretty safe."

Unfortunately, a police car chose that moment to go racing by, blues and twos blaring.

"If I don't see you to your door, I'll be awake all night, wondering if you made it home safe. Please, for me."

How could she resist a plea like that? And what other things would she concede in this marriage?

Chapter Three

"Are you mad? I go to Spain for two weeks and come back to find you've agreed to marry a total stranger?" Olivia shouted to be heard above the noise of the treadmills they were both on. "This from the woman who hasn't had a serious boyfriend ever! Never in a gazillion years would I have thought you, of all people, would do something so … so … outrageous." Olivia slowed her machine to a walk and stared at Sophia.

Sophia slowed down as well, wiping her face and neck with her towel. Having said it out loud, it did sound outrageous. How could she explain how sensible and reasonable it felt, at least when she was with Luca?

"It's not complete madness," she began. "Luca is … well, he's different from any other man I've met. More importantly, this is an amazing opportunity. I can leave my past and all the horrific memories behind and start a new life in a new country. I'm tired of working my butt off for nothing. This way I can get a degree and make something of myself. Make sure my children have a decent life. He's a good guy, so stop looking so worried."

Olivia stopped her treadmill and put her hand on Sophia's. "What about love?"

Sophia hit the stop button and stepped off the machine. "I don't want love. Love is a huge disappointment." She took a sip of water to clear her throat. "All I need is someone I can respect, especially if it means I don't have to worry about paying the rent or putting food on the table. Do you think that makes me a gold digger, or worse?" She moved over to the mat area to do some stretches. Olivia followed.

"You're asking me? I think trophy wife is a legitimate career choice. Marrying for money isn't always bad—unless you intend to divorce him after a few years and take everything you can get. People get married for a variety of reasons; who's to say what the right ones are? My worry is that you're a loving person, Sophia. What if eventually you want more from this marriage than just financial security?" Olivia started with a sun salutation stretch, ignoring the man on the rowing machine who stopped to watch her.

As a model, Olivia was used to people gawking at her. Although, even if she wasn't in front of a camera all day, at five foot nine, dark skinned with luxurious deep brown, spiral curls and a body that would have made Marilyn Munroe jealous, she still would have gotten a lot of attention. Sophia didn't envy her beauty, knowing at times it was more of a curse. What wasn't fair was that when Olivia worked out she glowed, unlike Sophia, who resembled a boiled lobster.

Sophia shrugged. "We plan on having children. I can give all my love to them."

Olivia switched to the downward dog position. "Love of children and love of a good man are two entirely different things. Still, it's a big risk. What if he turns out to be an axe murderer, or even worse, lousy in bed?"

Sophia's tree pose collapsed as she burst into laughter. "Olivia, you have the most bizarre priorities." She could always trust her friend to look at things from a different angle, especially when she was upside down.

"That doesn't answer whether he's good in bed." Olivia winked before resuming her concerned expression.

"Well, I don't have anyone to compare him to, do I? So it's a moot point."

A mischievous grin split her friend's face. "I think you should sample his wares, especially if he's as delicious as you describe."

"What makes you think I didn't?"

This time Olivia crumpled onto her mat in laughter. "I know you, my friend. If you'd shagged him, you wouldn't be so casually discussing his financial assets."

"He didn't make any moves on me," Sophia confessed. "After he walked me home, he just kissed me on the cheek and said goodnight." For the first time in her life she'd felt protected. Someone cared enough to see her safely home. It was an intoxicating sensation.

"He's not gay, is he? Is this marriage an elaborate ruse to hide his homosexuality from his family?" The look of horror on Olivia's face had Sophia laughing again.

"He's not gay. He was being a gentleman." She ignored Olivia's snort. "He told me up front he wants children, so there will be sex at some point in the marriage." She couldn't believe she was having this conversation, in public.

"And what do you, my virginal friend, think of that?"

"I, uh, I try not to," she lied. Truth was she'd thought of little else, especially after each phone call from Luca over the past two weeks. Must be something about his voice, so intimate in her ear, that stirred the woman in her. "I plan to lie back and think of England."

"Sweetie, if you can think at all, then it's no good," Olivia replied. "Seriously, you know nothing about Luca's life in Italy. What if he says he's this important property developer, but he really lives in a bedsit and expects you to earn your keep?"

"I looked him up on the Internet. Plus, my boss has known him a long time. Mr. Bodman said Luca is honorable, trustworthy, and considered a pillar of the Italian property development business." In fact, Mr. Bodman had waxed lyrical on Luca's virtues for some time.

Olivia put her hand on Sophia's again. "So you're really getting married on Thursday?"

"Yes, the sixteen-day waiting period will be up then. Luca is coming over in the morning, and we're flying to Milan in the afternoon. It's just going to be a small registry office wedding followed by lunch. I'm hoping you'll act as my witness?"

"Of course I will. You know I'll always be there for you. Is your family coming?"

"You're all the family I need."

"Sophia, you're getting married. Don't you think your parents have a right to know?"

"No. They gave up their right to know what was

happening in my life long ago." She shifted on her mat.

Olivia tilted her head to one side. "What about James? You still see your brother occasionally."

Sophia shook her head. "If I tell James, he'll feel obligated to tell my parents or my sister. I've let him know I'm taking a job in Italy and will be sending him money to finish his college course. I'll introduce the family to Luca when I think the time is right." She crossed her arms over her chest and considered getting on the elliptical to work off the surge of adrenaline racing through her.

Olivia opened her mouth but appeared to change her mind about what she was going to say. "Well, if you need another witness, Stuart is available. He lost his job again."

Sophia raised her eyebrows but didn't make any further comment. Olivia's boyfriends invariably turned out to be losers, but she'd have to wait for her friend to come to that realization herself.

"As long as he can spell his name, that's all I need."

Olivia glanced at the clock on the gym wall. "I better go. I've got to be up early tomorrow and if I show up with bags under my eyes I'll never hear the end of it. What time on Thursday? Unless you come to your senses in the meantime."

"I am being sensible, and nine o'clock at my flat."

Sophia hugged her friend tightly. They'd saved each other's lives—no marriage would come between that bond. But she had to look to the future … and bury her past.

• • •

Thursday was bright and clear, and for once Sophia got out of bed even before her alarm went off, rather than hitting the snooze button two or three times. She was barely out of the shower when the buzzer to her flat sounded. It couldn't be Olivia, as she had a key and would let herself in. A shiver raced up her spine at the thought it might be Luca, but he would be more than an hour early. She pulled on a short satin dressing gown—another second-hand store find like the dresses she wore to work—and hurried to answer the door.

A courier stood on the step with two large boxes, a clipboard, and a smile spreading across his face, no doubt at the sight of her scantily clad body. After signing the delivery slip, she raced back upstairs to her flat and hastily opened the biggest box first.

Inside was the most beautiful wedding gown she'd ever seen. It was Grecian in style, sleeveless with inch wide straps and a V at the front and back. There was a band of crystals just under the bust, then it fell in soft waves of ivory silk to the floor. At the bottom of the box was a pair of silver, strappy sandals with three-inch heels. The second box contained a fabulous bouquet of red roses, which filled the room with a lovely scent.

As she was holding the dress up to herself, remarking on the perfect fit, Olivia opened the door and stepped through.

"Wow, that dress is exquisite! Where on earth did you get the money for that?"

"Luca sent it, along with a wedding bouquet. Isn't it

fabulous?"

"With a dress like that, if you don't marry him, I will." Olivia teasingly pulled the dress out of her hands and held it up to herself.

"If you wear it, you'll need a police escort," Sophia replied, pointing out her friend's more ample assets.

"Come on. Let's doll you up. Luca will hardly recognize you when he arrives."

"As we've only seen each other three times, he may not recognize me anyway," she said wryly. She sat down so Olivia could brush out her hair and put it up.

"Does that mean I could knock you out and take your place, and he wouldn't notice?"

She looked at Olivia in the mirror. As her closest friend and better than family, Sophia would deny her nothing. Except the man who was soon to be her husband. Luca was her best chance at a better life and she had to seize it.

A large roller suitcase and a small carry-on bag stood by the door. A few cardboard boxes were stacked in a corner. Sophia's shelves were bare of the little knick-knacks that had made the small flat home. "The rent is paid up to the end of the month, and I told the landlord that you would take the boxes away," she said.

"So this is really it. You're going and not coming back." Olivia's voice caught on the last word.

"Please, Olivia. No tears today. Today is for celebration. It's a new start."

"Let's get you gorgeous for your new start, then." Olivia wiped her hand across her cheek, then set to work.

She swept Sophia's hair up in a loose twist, with

curls at her temples and along her nape, and one long curl nestled in the back V of her dress, making it look like it had come loose in a passionate embrace. Sophia generally wore very little makeup—a dusting of eye shadow and a bit of mascara—but Olivia made her eyes seem huge and greener than usual. She painted Sophia's mouth a deep rose, making her lips look like they had just been kissed

"My God, Olivia, who the hell is that?" She was so used to looking in the mirror, fixing what was obviously out of place, and walking away, that she never even dreamed she could look like this. "Having a best friend who's a model really comes in handy," she said, still staring. "Why haven't you haven't made me look like this before?"

"You've never wanted to get all dolled up before, said you were the plain-Jane type. But this is your wedding day and you only get married once, provided you do it right the first time. Besides, I didn't want to have to deal with that kind of competition," Olivia replied, indicating the reflection.

The sound of the buzzer drowned out their laughter. "That must be Stuart. He wasn't ready when I left this morning. He went on a bit of a bender last night."

Unable to sit still, Sophia went over to the window as Olivia ran down the three flights of stairs to let in Stuart. A limo drew up and Luca stepped out, surveying the building in front of him. Her heart went into overdrive. The black suit, white shirt, and azure tie made him look suave yet powerful. The reality of what she was doing finally hit her, and she leaned into the wall for support.

Luca looked up, and she was startled by the intensity on his face. Her heart rate calmed. She might be making the worst mistake of her life, marrying a man she barely knew, but it was time she took life by the scruff of the neck and shook it till it gave her what she wanted. She wanted the opportunities Luca Castellioni's money would give her. It didn't hurt that it all came wrapped in a gorgeous package.

Olivia stepped into her view of the pavement, and the two shook hands, but Luca displayed no undue interest in her friend. In fact his eyes returned to her window within seconds. Sophia gave a brief wave before dropping the curtain and had a final glance around her bedsit. It was time to start again.

Stuart appeared a moment later, grunted "hello," grabbed her bag, and headed back down the stairs.

Olivia poked her head around the door. "Okay, I don't think you're crazy now. But the man is intense. Are you sure you're up for this? I can tell him if you've changed your mind…"

Sophia squared her shoulders and took a deep breath. "I'm ready," she declared.

Arm in arm, the two women descended the stairs. Luca and Stuart were engaged in an animated discussion about football and at first didn't notice their arrival. When Luca caught sight of her, he stopped mid-sentence, his arm flung wide in a dramatic gesture, his mouth open. Her mouth went dry and the air whooshed out of her lungs at the look of pure lust in his eyes before he recovered his expression. She forced herself to remain where she was and not race back up the stairs. Maybe she wasn't quite ready for everything this marriage entailed. But there was no turning back now. She squared her shoulders and continued walking toward Luca.

"*Bellissima*," he whispered, as he took her hand in his. His voice was husky and he seemed lost for words. Clearing his throat, he added, "Our appointment is in forty minutes. We must go soon. You need anything else?"

Appointment, not wedding. She looked back at the building that had been her home for the past four years. The red paint on the bricks had faded to a dull pink. The draughty windows would be chilling someone else in future. It had been the first place she could call her own, but aside from a few laughs with Olivia, it held no fond memories—only worries about paying the rent and what the future held.

"No, I have everything." She lifted her chin and tried to smile. "I packed a set of clothes in my carry-on bag so I can change after … lunch." The last word came out a bit strangled; she couldn't quite keep all the apprehension out of her voice. He smiled and squeezed her hand in support.

"Shall we go then?" Luca said, ushering them into the limo. His hand found its way to the small of her back, sending a slow-burning heat up her spine. Sitting next to him in the car, their thighs touching, she fidgeted as tingles radiated throughout her entire body.

They arrived at the registry office, and all too soon, she found herself standing next to Luca. He held both her hands and stared into her eyes. In a deep, husky voice he promised to, "protect, respect and care for Sophia for the rest of my life." For a brief second, she almost believed in love. Then Olivia's boyfriend yawned loudly, bringing Sophia to her senses.

She cleared her throat and her voice only shook a little as she promised to "honor, respect and care for Luca for the rest of my life."

She'd done it. She'd really, finally closed a door on her past and started a new life. Gone was Sophia Stevens. The pain of the past could now be buried under a new identity, a new life.

She was Sophia Castellioni.

The registrar made his final pronouncements about the legality of their union, making a small effort to sound like he hadn't said the exact same words a thousand times already. "You may kiss the bride," he finally declared.

Luca's mouth descended, in slow motion. As his warm lips touched hers, a white hot flame burst to life behind her eyes. Before she got used to the sensation, he pulled back an inch. Instinctively, she opened her lips to protest. In the next instant he pulled her hard against his tall, muscular body. The gentle, just-married kiss transformed to a full on assault of her senses. The flame behind her eyes became an all-out inferno that threatened to sear her mind.

Olivia's fake cough brought her back to reality with a bump. Luca slowly relaxed his grip, holding her against him while she regained her balance. His skin was flushed and his breathing rapid, echoing her own. With a little shake of his head, he turned to the registrar and thanked him for the ceremony.

"I know this is not the wedding you probably dreamed of," he said after they signed the required documentation. "I have asked a photographer to take a few photos. Would it be too much if I ask you to pretend we are in love? You see, my mother will want some pictures…" He shrugged, a gesture that said where his mother was concerned, he would do anything to make her happy.

"Of course. I'm very good at pretending," she replied.

The photographer took several dozen shots. Luca holding her, gazing into her eyes, kissing her lightly. Anyone who saw the photos would believe this was a love match.

When they made their way to the waiting limo, Sophia was lightheaded. She put it down to the brevity of the ceremony and the sudden realization that she now was married to Luca, and not the memory of his just-married kiss that caused her confusion. If just the touch of his lips on hers had this effect, what would it be like tonight—tonight when his lips were free to explore? He said he'd wait for children, but would he wait to consummate their marriage? Did *she* want to wait? And what would he say when he saw her scars?

Olivia sidled up to her and whispered in her ear, "I seriously doubt you'll be thinking of England tonight." The comment, so close to her own thoughts, sent a shiver through her whole body.

Chapter Four

"We are now descending into Milan Malpensa airport," the captain announced over the intercom. "Flight attendants, please prepare the cabin for landing."

Luca glanced over at Sophia as she brought her seatback into the upright position. She looked tired but didn't seem unusually nervous, despite this being her first time flying. He wished he could read her, but she was an enigma. Her serenity in the unusual circumstances was a bit disconcerting. As they'd left the hotel after lunch, Sophia had hugged Olivia, then put her hand on his arm and walked out without looking back. He had no idea what she thought of their quick marriage. But his imagination was in top form just thinking about the possibilities of their wedding night, while his wife looked as though a river of ice flowed through her veins.

She hadn't even batted an eyelash when he'd apologized about the need to work on the flight. She'd simply smiled and reclined and closed her eyes. Putting his papers back in his briefcase, he stowed it under the seat in front. He took hold of her hand on the armrest between them—to give her some support if she was nervous about the landing, of course—and was rewarded with a shy smile. It was a new feeling for him. Sure, he had enjoyed his share of female companionship over the years, yet he had never felt a longing to simply touch someone. It wasn't something that pleased him.

Thirty minutes later, Sophia's eyes widened as the valet handed over the keys to his Maserati GranTurismo. Luca opened the passenger door for her and couldn't help grinning at the surprised look on her face. "This is my favorite toy," he remarked as he slid behind the wheel. Her small, delicate hands ran over the butter-soft leather seats and along the dash. His mouth went dry as he imagined those same hands caressing his body. "I have a more practical vehicle, a Land Rover, for visiting job sites. This makes being stuck in traffic bearable. Do you drive?"

"No, I never learned. And looking at this traffic, I don't think I want to learn in Italy."

"City traffic takes getting used to," he acknowledged. "Out in the country where I—*we* live, it is much easier to drive. I will teach you."

"Maybe when I adjust to the cars on the wrong side of the road," she replied quietly. She stared out the window at the passing scenery, seeming so calm, serene.

"It is such a beautiful country," she commented as they left the motorway and started to drive through the village. "I've hardly been out of London. Have you always lived in this part of Italy?"

"Yes, I was born not far from where we now live. My mother is originally from Sardinia, so I went there for summer holidays while my grandparents were alive. Then I lived in Milan in my twenties. When the villa came on the market, I jumped at the chance to buy it. Of course, it was in a derelict state, and it took almost a year to restore. I've only lived in it for six months. I'm hoping you will have some suggestions on how to make it feel more like a home. Perhaps your interior design skills will help."

"How did you know I was studying interior design?" Sophia's eyes narrowed.

"Olivia mentioned it. I don't remember if it was before or after she told me that she would hunt me down and castrate me if I ever hurt you," he replied, with a mock shiver.

Sophia laughed, finally "Olivia is a bit protective."

"Protecting you is my job now. But she seems like a good friend."

"Olivia's the best. Would you mind if she came for a visit in a couple of months?"

"She can come any time you wish. There's plenty of room." He drove through the new steel gates and pulled into the semicircle driveway.

"This … this is your house?"

"Our house," he corrected as he stopped the car. Her reaction surprised him. He knew she'd married him for his money, and it seemed, the chance to leave London, but clearly she hadn't expected this level of wealth. It suited him that she'd been easy to persuade. But at the back of his mind, he wondered what had made her desperate enough to accept his proposal.

They had a lifetime to get to know each other's secrets—starting tonight. His blood rushed to his groin as it had when he'd first seen her in her wedding gown. Never having experienced such instant lust before, he was as intrigued as disconcerted.

He dragged his mind from the bedroom and helped

her out of the low-slung sports car. "Come, I'll introduce you to Maria and Vittore." His hand found its way to the small of her back of its own volition.

"Who are they?" Sophia looked around as if she couldn't believe what she was seeing.

"Maria is the cook and Vittore is the gardener. They live on-site. The girl who cleans comes in from the village each day."

"You have staff?"

"Of course, you don't think I brought you here to clean and cook, do you?"

"It's a good thing, because I can only cook beans on toast and jacket potatoes."

"That does not even qualify as cooking." He winked.

• • •

Sophia wiped damp palms on her trousers. *Staff?* What did she know about directing staff? And what would they think of her, the bought bride who knew nothing of their language or culture?

They climbed the five stone stairs to the massive double front doors. Luca had to take his hand from her back to open the door with a massive ornate key.

"Shall I carry you across the threshold?"

She smiled at his effort to pretend this was a proper marriage. "I don't think that will be necessary."

He looked almost disappointed. "Welcome to your new home." He flung his arm wide and waited for her to enter first.

The entrance was wide and tiled in white marble. A round, wooden table stood in the center of the room with a large vase of fresh flowers. A curved staircase on the left side of the hallway led to an upstairs gallery. The walls were painted a pale cream and dotted with sepia-toned pictures of vineyards and olive groves. Understated elegance came to mind, but no hint of warmth or comfort.

"I will give you the quick tour and you can wander around at your leisure later." Luca opened a door on the right, revealing a sitting room that looked stiff and uncomfortable. There was no glimpse of his personality. He continued through glass doors from the sitting room to a large dining room, furnished with a heavy oak table and high-back chairs. The furniture would fit in a medieval castle—a modern Italian villa, not so much. From the dining room they returned to the entrance hall through an arched doorway.

"That door leads to the kitchen," Luca said, as though that part of the house was some foreign territory to which visas were seldom issued.

They crossed to a paneled door that led to another sitting room. This one was a lot cozier and the first room in the house where Sophia could imagine spending any amount of time. She pictured herself in winter on the large, overstuffed cream sofa, snuggled under a blanket, reading a book with a fire crackling in the tall fireplace across the room. Or better yet, snuggled in Luca's arms watching the firelight play across his handsome face. To distract herself from the fantasy, she moved over to the mantel to look at the photos displayed there.

"My mother," Luca said, coming to stand close behind her, "taken on her recent wedding day. I've not told her about our marriage yet. There will be plenty of time for her to meet you later."

She moved the frame so it was straight on the mantel and glanced up at Luca. Had he not told his mother because their marriage was simply a business arrangement to him, a transaction like purchasing a piece of property? Whatever the reason, she was relieved she didn't have to deal with a mother-in-law straight away.

"Let me introduce you to Maria." He took her hand in his and walked through to the kitchen.

A couple were sat at the table, having a hot beverage and a slice of cake, but jumped up as Luca entered. A flurry of Italian followed, and Sophia took the opportunity to look around. The kitchen was gorgeous. Brass-bottomed pots hung from a rack above the marble-topped island. Bottles of oil with various peppers and spices inside were lined up on the counter like soldiers waiting for a call to duty. And the smell—her stomach rumbled with one sniff. The scent of a hundred homemade meals, cooked with love and attention, lingered in the air. She'd been too nervous to eat at lunchtime, and her body took the opportunity to remind her.

The couple approached and she shook hands with the elderly man. He looked about a hundred years old, but his handshake was firm, and he had a sparkle in his eye as he smiled at her. His wife was delightfully round, and rather than shaking Sophia's outstretched hand, Maria enveloped her in a hug, kissing her on both cheeks while whispering something in Italian that she couldn't understand. At least it sounded welcoming.

Luca's mobile phone rang. He silenced it, then turned to Sophia with an apologetic smile. "Sorry to cut short the tour, but I have a deal closing this afternoon. I have to make a few phone calls now, if you'll excuse me. Feel free to wander around. Do you want something to eat before dinner? Maria will be happy to make you a snack."

"Perhaps a slice of cake and a coffee?"

Luca translated her request and Maria bustled over to the counter to cut a slice of cake. "Unfortunately, neither of them speak any English. But I'm sure you'll find a way to communicate. Dinner will be at 8:00 pm. I'll see you in the front room then?"

"Okay," Sophia replied. She took a deep breath to ease the pressure in her chest. Well, he'd warned her that business was his first priority. She might as well get used to it.

Luca kissed her briefly on the cheek before turning on his heel and leaving the room. She smiled at the elderly couple and took a seat at the table. Because she was unable to communicate with her companions, silence loomed long and large in the beautiful kitchen. Their faces were kindly as they sat with her, but she could sense their curiosity. It wasn't every day their boss went out in the morning and returned a few hours later with a bride.

Sophia finished the delicious lemon cake and coffee in record time. She needed a few minutes alone to process the day's events. With a stammered, "*Grazie*," she left the room.

She might as well explore. Maybe she should leave a trail of shiny pebbles to find her way back. Wandering back to the base of the stairs, she heard Luca's deep voice in the room to the left. She poked her head around the door and discovered a massive office with one wall completely covered in bookshelves. A huge oak desk was piled with papers and an array of three monitors. Luca stood looking out the window, his back to the door, a phone held to his ear.

"Chet, I apologize that I didn't return your call earlier. I was in London concluding some business there… Three weeks? Excellent. I will make arrangements for us to visit the properties I mentioned to you. Have you received the letter of intent? … Good, as soon as you return a signed copy, I will forward to you the details…"

Sophia retreated and returned to the entryway. Her stomach roiled and for a second she thought she might lose the lemon cake she'd just enjoyed. Their marriage was a business transaction to Luca. The late night phone calls, the flowers, the beautiful wedding dress he'd sent had been the sweetener to seal the deal. She'd started to believe that maybe he cared for her. Now she knew better. She was only another piece in his property portfolio.

Her suitcase sat beside the front door. She lugged it up the stairs as quietly as possible, not wanting to disturb Luca. A house this big had to have a variety of bedrooms. She was going to choose hers. If Luca wanted her in his bed, he'd have to make an appointment.

She left her case at the top of the stairs and started opening doors. The first room she tried was obviously the master. A huge, four-poster king-sized bed dominated the room. She quickly closed the door and strode toward the other end of the hallway. There were several smaller bedrooms, decorated in pale shades of blue, green and pink. She was a bit like Goldilocks, searching for the room that was just right.

At the end of the corridor, she opened a door to a bright room decorated in hues of yellow. A large, shiny brass bed with a white chenille bedspread sat against the opposite wall. Sophia looked around the room in appreciation. It was bigger than her whole flat in London. Double doors led out onto a balcony. On the other side of the room, another door was open, through which she could see a large tub and shower enclosure. This was it. She retrieved her suitcase from the top of the stairs and then unpacked her few belongings.

It was only six o'clock, so she stepped out onto the balcony. The house was so cold, the air-conditioning set on high, it was wonderful to move into the warm, spring evening. The scents of thousands of blossoms wafted up, surrounding her.

Leaning on the deck railing, she checked out the gardens. The flower beds were immaculate, well-loved by Vittore, no doubt. The house and grounds were more than she ever imagined. She couldn't help feeling, however, that something was missing. It was more than just badly chosen furniture and a lack of personal touches. The villa lacked the very essence of what it took to make a house a home. The word love came to mind, but she pushed it aside. She'd deal with the décor later. For now she had to work out how she was going to tell Luca he wasn't getting any action tonight.

As she washed and changed for dinner she caught sight of her scars in the mirror, a reminder of her past. It was the invisible scars of feeling worthless and helpless that still plagued her, although she hid them as she did her visible marks. But every once in a while they'd surface, and she'd be a frightened girl unsure of her place in the world. So until she was certain Luca saw her as a person, not a thing, she would sleep alone.

At five minutes to eight, Sophia stepped into the front sitting room. She'd changed into a green dress that echoed the color of her eyes. Her hair was still up from the wedding, and by reapplying her lipstick and refreshing her makeup, she felt she made a presentable picture.

The room was empty so she wandered over to the front window. Luca's car sat in the drive like an exclamation point to the luxury of the house. Seven years ago, when she'd run from her parents' home, she'd lived on the streets, often sleeping behind a dumpster. This new start would bring no such discomfort. Still, she felt more out of place now than she had as a homeless teen.

The hairs on the back of her neck stood on end and she turned to find Luca watching her. He stared at her for a moment more, and when his gaze fixed on her hands, she realized she'd been pleating the fabric between her fingers.

"*Buona sera, bellissima.* Would you like a drink?"

He walked over to the drinks tray set on the sideboard. He hadn't changed out of his suit but had removed his tie and undone a couple of buttons on his shirt. He looked sexy and powerful, and she had to clear her throat before she could speak.

"Um, no thank you. Perhaps I'll have a glass of wine with dinner." She was already dizzy enough with him near.

"Relax, *cara*. I'm not going to eat you." His lips said the words but the heat in his eyes as they roved over her body belied his statement. Warmth flushed through her, settling in her lower abdomen, and for a moment she rethought her plan of having her own bedroom.

Maria entered the dining room and placed a large platter on the table. She opened the glass doors into the sitting room and said something in Italian to Luca before leaving.

"Dinner is ready," Luca translated. "Shall we eat?" Already his hand had found its way to the small of her back and was steering her toward the table through the open doors. He pulled out her chair and waited for her to be seated before sitting at the head of the table. Maria returned and placed a tureen on the table and quietly said something to Luca as she left the room.

"Please, help yourself," he said as he removed the cover from the platter. The first tray contained an assortment of cold meats, pickled artichokes, olives, and breads while the tureen held minestrone soup. He poured her a glass of wine as she filled her plate. The delicious soup had clearly never seen the inside of a can. The aroma of fresh herbs and homegrown vegetables impressed Sophia with each spoonful. As she finished, Maria returned, carrying a heaped bowl of pasta, which she placed on the table and then spoke quietly to Luca before retreating.

"I tried to learn a few Italian phrases before I came, but obviously I have a lot to learn. Did I do something wrong?" Sophia inquired.

"Not at all. Maria was commenting on your good appetite."

"The food is so delicious. I don't think I've ever tasted anything so good."

"I will pass on your compliment when she brings the main course in," he replied, a hint of laughter in his eyes. The warm, human Luca was back. He'd left the businessman in the office.

"The main course? What is this then?" Sophia pointed at the heaped bowl of pasta.

"This is the second course. First was antipasto and soup, then pasta. The main course is *cotoletta*, which is breaded veal, and polenta, I believe she said. Then dessert and cheeses and fresh fruit, if you wish."

"You eat like this every night? I'm amazed you're not thirty stone!" She admired his lean, muscular form.

"I rarely eat at home. Maria is trying to impress you with a special meal."

"Well, I am impressed, but please tell her that I can't eat like this every night. I'm used to having a sandwich for dinner. One course is all I need, if that. If you don't eat at home, why do you have a cook?"

"Maria and Vittore came with the house, so to speak. When I bought the place the previous owner asked if I would hire them. They have lived and worked here for almost forty years. During the renovation, Maria kept the workers well fed. This was my crew's favorite job site," he explained.

"As you have a cook, cleaner, and gardener, I guess there's not much for me to do around the house," she mused. How was she going to fill her days? Having worked two, sometimes three, jobs at a time for the last five years, and studied or done charity work in any spare time she had, she wasn't used to being idle.

"You'll find something to fill your time. Milan is one of the world's fashion capitals. I'm sure you'll enjoy shopping," Luca replied.

"I suppose so," she agreed absently. She wasn't much of a shopper. Then again she'd never had money to shop with before. One thing she really needed to do was learn Italian. She couldn't sit in stilted silence with the cook and gardener while Luca was away at work all day.

The rest of the meal passed in pleasant conversation. Luca told her about the state of the property when he first bought it and the renovation process. "I didn't choose the furniture or decorative items. So if there is anything you want to change, do so. I'm not attached to anything, except my study," he said.

When Maria brought in the dessert and coffee, Sophia thanked her for the delicious dinner. Marie beamed as she left the room. But it also signaled the end of the meal. Sophia's hand shook as she stirred some sugar into her coffee.

"I think you've made a conquest there," Luca noted.

"Shall we have our coffee in the sitting room?" He rose and picked up her cup.

Sophia sat on the bright red sofa and tried to get comfortable. The seat was too wide, so she couldn't lean against the back without having her feet stick straight out like a child's. And it was so low to the floor that if she sat forward her legs splayed out like a crushed spider. She wondered if it was bought for no other reason than because it was the most expensive one in the store.

Luca sat next to her and handed her the coffee. Tangible electricity flowed between them. The butterflies in her stomach turned to sparrows and threatened to bring up the delicious dinner with their out-of-formation flying.

Glancing at Luca's face, she recognized the raw passion and stared at the coffee cup in her hands. She started to speak, cleared her throat, and tried again. "Um, Luca, there is something I should tell you…"

He looked at her, his eyebrows raised, as if wondering what terrible secret she could be about to reveal.

"I'm a virgin—I haven't had, um, sex before," she blurted out. "And, well, we've not really spent a lot of time together. I want to wait until I know you better before we share a bed. I've put my things in the yellow bedroom."

Chapter Five

Luca swallowed. Disappointment warred with elation. He wouldn't be an Italian male if he wasn't pleased to know his wife had never been with another man. But all day he'd been anticipating tonight, when he could remove the pins from her hair and watch it tumble down her naked back. Feather kisses down her long, graceful neck until he came to her pert breasts... Perhaps if they repeated the kiss they'd exchanged at the registry office, Sophia would change her mind about delaying their wedding night.

No. She needed time and he would respect her wishes. They had years and years together. He could wait—if it wasn't too long. The little voice in his head gave a rueful laugh. It seemed his rule on not sleeping with married women extended to his own wife.

Hopefully, the delay was only a temporary setback and would be resolved before the Wilkinses arrived. It hadn't felt right to tell Chet he'd not returned his calls sooner because he was getting married. There was already going to be enough speculation by his friends and associates about his quick marriage. Most, he knew, would assume Sophia was pregnant. In a way it would have made the whole situation more understandable. No one would believe he hadn't even slept with her yet. He'd have to rely on her acting ability to see them through any difficulty. She'd been amazing during the wedding photos, even had him believing for a moment theirs was a love match. Even more surprising was the fact he hadn't had any difficulty pretending to be enamored with her, either.

Now, gazing at her beautiful face, he doused his desire. "I understand. This has all been rather sudden. *When* I make you my wife in more than name, it must be something you want as much as I do." He leaned over and kissed her on the lips. Liquid heat shot through his veins. *Control yourself, it's just a kiss,* the voice in his head tried to reason. He resisted the urge to taste her deeper, or allow his hands to explore her soft curves. With a low groan, he pulled away.

Sophia's chest rose and fell rapidly and a dazed expression clouded her eyes. "I'm tired. I think I'll go to bed now. See you in the morning?" Her voice was husky.

Dio, he hoped it wouldn't be long before they shared a bed. "I must leave very early for work tomorrow. I will try to be home for dinner. So I will see you then. If you need anything, call me at my office." No wonder she didn't want to sleep with him. He was a boring businessman. Problem was, he didn't know how to be anything else.

• • •

Sophia opened her eyes and had a moment's panic. The sun was shining on her face and her first thought was that she was back sleeping on the street. This bed was way too comfortable for any makeshift mattress, however. A flash of gold on her finger returned her heart rate to normal. This was her future; she was no longer mired in the past.

She stretched in the large, luxurious bed, surprised she'd slept so deeply. After Luca's goodnight kiss, she thought she'd toss and turn for hours, wondering whether she'd made the right decision. Maybe sex was like removing a plaster; you had to get it over quickly before you thought about it too much. She could almost hear Olivia's laugh at the analogy.

It wasn't so much the actual physical deed that churned her stomach. She'd read enough to know that consummation was supposed to be rather pleasant. And Luca certainly looked the part of a passionate, caring lover. No, it was the emotional aspect, the letting someone see her—scars and all—that scared the pants back on her. She didn't trust easily, and for sex you had to trust. Or get blind, stupid drunk. That was always an option.

Twenty minutes later, she descended the stairs, hoping to sneak into the kitchen and find a bowl of cereal or a piece of toast. It was after ten o'clock; she hadn't slept so late in years. Opening the kitchen door, she almost passed out from the sight of all the food. Baked goods, boiled eggs, an assortment of deli meats, and fresh fruit were displayed on the table like a king's buffet. Despite having eaten a week's worth of food the night before, Sophia's stomach gurgled at the smell of the freshly baked muffins. She had to figure out a way to tell Maria not to cook so much or she would soon resemble an elephant.

Maria bustled over to her, wiping her hands on her apron, chattering away in Italian. Sophia sat in the chair Maria indicated and filled her plate. Forget shopping, she was going to be spending her days trying to work off all the food she consumed. As she ate, Maria talked, a happy buzz of conversation that evidently didn't require any input from Sophia. Finally she managed to make Maria understand that she couldn't eat another bite. But as she stood to take her dishes to the sink, Maria waved her away. She caught the words "signora," which she assumed meant her, and "no," which was obvious. Evidently, Luca's missus didn't do dishes.

With nothing else to keep her busy, she decided to explore the gardens. The sun warmed her, and the air was alive with the sounds of birds and various insects going about their daily business. Pausing for a moment, she listened for the noise of cars or other vehicles. There weren't any. She couldn't remember the last time she had been anywhere as peaceful. Determined not to spoil such a beautiful day with worries, she pushed aside thoughts of her marriage and let her senses dwell on the tranquility of the place. London seemed a very long way away.

Behind the pool and tennis court, screened off by a massive hedge, were two decent-sized, stone cottages. Walking past them on the manicured pathway, Sophia came across a rotunda set within a topiary and rose garden. Beyond that, she also discovered a couple of derelict buildings at the back of the land that had not been restored and were crammed with bits of furniture, statues, and other odds and ends. It appeared the pieces had been found during the reconstruction work and tossed there to be sorted out later. She made a mental note to come back on another day and see what treasures she could turn up.

A small pond, at the far corner of the estate, was home to a couple of ducks that quacked loudly as she approached, warning her away from their nest. As she sauntered back toward the house, she saw Vittore planting seeds in a bare area of an otherwise large, lush vegetable patch. Maria was cutting herbs and putting them in a wicker basket. Both called out "*buongiorno*" to her. She waved at them in reply.

Not wanting to go back inside and waste a glorious day, she decided to wander into the village. She'd noted an old church and some other interesting buildings as they drove past yesterday on their way from the airport.

The village was larger than she'd thought, with narrow, twisting, cobblestone streets that turned into even smaller alleyways. An old church was at the center, with a small piazza in front. Several older men were drinking coffee at a café and looked her up and down as she passed.

She strolled in and out of the shops and admired the ancient buildings and architecture. Stopping by a fountain, she trailed her fingers in the cool water. There were a few coins at the bottom, and she imagined a lonely girl standing there, tossing in her euro and wishing for love. She turned away before the image of her own face appeared in place of the girl's.

Her stomach growled and she checked her watch, surprised to discover it was already four o'clock. She managed to make her way back to the old church, but from there she had no idea which of the twisty streets led back to the house. Wandering down a few roads, she searched for something familiar. Her feet were sore and her mouth parched. Intending just a quick exploration of the village, she hadn't thought to bring her purse, so she couldn't even purchase a drink.

She went into a café and asked if anyone knew the way to Villa Castellioni, the name that she had seen printed on the outside of the gate to the house. Unfortunately, Sophia couldn't understand the directions the proprietress gave her.

"Are you trying to find Villa Castellioni?" a deep male voice asked. She turned around to discover a tall, blonde man with sky-blue eyes.

"Yes, do you know it?" She was grateful to find someone who spoke English at least.

"Is it that beautiful, big house just outside the village that was renovated last year?"

"I guess so. I mean, I know it was renovated recently. I only came here yesterday, so I'm not familiar with all the houses in the area," she replied.

"Jonathan Davis," he said, extending his hand. "I'm fixing up a place not too far from that villa. If you want, I can give you a lift."

"I am Sophia Stevens—I mean Sophia Castellioni," she corrected herself. "Sorry, I was married yesterday. I'm still getting used to the name change."

"Married yesterday and your husband has already let you wander off and get lost?"

"Luca had to go in to work." Sophia defended her

husband. She knew what she was getting into, kind of, when she married him. But she didn't want others to think he'd abandoned her. If they had a real marriage... For that to ever happen, she had to get home first. Her feet throbbed, and she was so thirsty she didn't think she could manage the walk back to the villa.

She stared at Jonathan's face. Her instincts had never steered her wrong when she'd lived on the streets. The man in front of her displayed none of the signs of someone with malicious intent. And if he were a crazed, psychotic killer, at least she wouldn't leave Luca heartbroken. He could probably pop back to London and pick up another woman. Aside from Olivia, she wouldn't leave anyone behind. "I will take that lift, if you don't mind."

Jonathan led her to a dilapidated truck with a load of building supplies in the back. He negotiated the narrow, winding streets with ease, and soon they were pulling up to the gates of the house.

"Would you like to come in for a drink?" Sophia invited. It seemed rude to just leave after he'd rescued her.

"Sure. I'd love to see the renovation. I saw the villa in its original condition on the Internet when it was on the market. It sold before I moved to Italy."

"Oh, how long have you lived here?"

"Almost seven months. The renovation on your place was almost complete by the time I arrived."

"Well, the house itself is gorgeous. I'm not too sure about some of the furniture. It's not really in keeping with the style of the property," she commented. "In fact, when I was in the village I saw a beautiful sofa that would look brilliant in the front sitting room. It just needs to be reupholstered…"

Luca stood on the front step, raking a hand through his hair. He stopped as Jonathan's truck pulled up in front. His narrowed eyes searched the vehicle, and then her, as she jumped out of the passenger seat. He shoved both hands in his pockets, his face darkening as Jonathan got out, too.

As Sophia was about to introduce the two men, a tall, dark-haired woman came up behind Luca and put her arm through his. She was immaculately dressed in a gray, silk frock that hugged her luscious shape and ended mid-thigh, showing long, shapely legs.

"Hello, Luca," Sophia struggled to keep her voice even. "I didn't think you would be home yet. You said around dinner time."

"I finished earlier than I expected and came home to see my wife, thinking she would be lonely. I didn't know she would be wandering around with another man." Luca's voice was hard and there was no smile of greeting on his face.

"Oh, this is Jonathan Davis. He rescued me when I was lost in the village. He's fixing up a place not too far from here, so he offered to drive me home." She knew the words were coming out too fast, but she was fixated by the sight of the other woman's arm through Luca's. She'd never considered that perhaps her husband had a *lover*. "This is Isabella Carrero," Luca introduced the woman standing next to him. Removing his hand from his pocket, he unlinked arms with Isabella.

"I offered Jonathan a drink for rescuing me," Sophia explained as the Englishman climbed the stairs beside her.

"Yes, let us have drinks on the *terrazza*," Isabella said, as if she were the lady of the house. Her voice was deep and sultry, her Italian accent more pronounced than Luca's.

Luca led the way to the back of the house, taking Sophia's hand in his as she passed. She wondered whether the display of possessiveness was a message to Jonathan, or a ploy to try to pretend the Italian woman meant nothing to him.

The terrace was in the shade; however the heat of the day still radiated off the stone floor, making it warm and comfortable. Baskets of flowers filled the air with a sweet scent. Dark wicker chairs, with terracotta colored cushions, were spread out in a U shape, allowing all to enjoy the view of the gardens. Isabella took the seat next to Luca's, moving her chair closer to his. Sophia clenched her teeth, a slow burn starting in her stomach.

The peace and serenity of the gardens, which she'd enjoyed hours before, was shattered. How could she have been so stupid to believe Luca, a successful, not to mention gorgeous, man wouldn't have a woman or two in the background? He'd said there weren't any other women he would consider marrying, but that didn't preclude other relationships.

"So, you are renovating a house near here?" Luca's frosty tone hadn't warmed at all.

"Yes, nothing as grand as this, though. Your home is beautiful," Jonathan said.

"*Grazie,*" Luca answered.

Maria pushed a small drinks cart out onto the terrace and placed it near the chairs. Isabella jumped up and took over the role of hostess.

"What you like to drink, Sophia, Jonathan?" Isabella oozed confidence, sure of her place.

Luca frowned at Isabella. Was it because the other woman had paired Sophia's name with Jonathan's, or because his girlfriend was assuming a duty that should now be handled by his wife? Sophia was once again out of her depth, unsure of what to do.

"I'll have a glass of white wine," she answered, with as much composure as she could manage.

"A beer for me, if you have one," Jonathan replied.

Isabella poured the drinks and handed them out. She then mixed a martini for Luca, without even asking what he preferred.

"Sophia, you must talk to your husband. He says he does not want to bring you to my party tomorrow so you can meet our friends." A stabbing pain shot through Sophia's body, paralyzing her. Isabella's voice was silky, with no hint of jealousy, no concern for the agony her words caused. Isabella sat on the arm of Luca's chair, having abandoned her own after preparing the drinks. "No one will believe you are married if you keep her hidden away in this little village."

"I have no intention of keeping her hidden away," Luca assured them. "But I am sure Sophia wants to settle in before meeting a lot of people."

"No, you must introduce her right away," Isabella insisted. "Or people will wonder why you waited. They will be shocked, like me, to find you are married. They will think it is not a proper marriage."

"It is a very proper marriage," Luca replied. He took a large swallow of his drink. His knuckles showed white where he gripped the stem of the glass.

"Luca, imagine the party your mother will insist you have when she finds out about your wedding. If you tell her you have already had a party, then it will not be so bad. I am saving you, *caro*." Isabella smiled at everyone, smug satisfaction written across her face.

Luca seemed to think over the plan, glancing at Sophia as if to gauge her reaction. Without knowing her place in his life, she was unsure how forcefully to protest. She didn't want to start her marriage coming across as a diva.

"I don't have anything to wear," she interjected as Luca made no further comment. It was the only thing she could think of to stop this party idea. The last thing she needed was to be inspected by Luca's friends and acquaintances and found wanting—especially compared to Isabella.

"Ah, that is a little thing." Isabella dismissed her concern with a wave of a hand. "We can go shopping for a dress … and shoes," she said, glancing at Sophia's well-worn footwear. "You are working tomorrow, yes, Luca? Or are you a changed man now that you are married? Staying at home on a Saturday to be with your wife?"

"I do have to make some site visits tomorrow. But I was going to take Sophia with me so she can see some of the country."

"*Dai*, there is plenty of time for her to see the dusty roads and broken buildings you will show her. I am sure you can spare her for a day. Shopping is much more fun."

"I don't speak Italian. I won't be able to talk with anyone." She had to derail this party train before it crushed her.

"Most of our friends speak some English," Isabella said, blocking off that avenue of escape. "Perhaps your rescuer could come as well." She smiled at Jonathan, luring him into her web.

Jonathan sat there with a bemused expression on his face. "I am not sure I'd really fit in," he replied, pointing at his tattered jeans.

"Oh, please come," Sophia pleaded. If she was going to have to endure this party, it would be nice to have someone there for her.

Jonathan shrugged. "Alright then, I'll come. You have my mobile number, Sophia, you can text me the details. I must be off now, though. I have to unload my truck before dark."

"I'll show you out," Luca responded, a hint of a smile showing on his face at last.

● ● ●

Luca returned and stopped at the entrance to the terrace, allowing himself a moment to enjoy Sophia unobserved. She hadn't gotten publicly upset when Isabella put her arm through his, although he'd noticed that she'd narrowed her eyes. Sophia hadn't liked it. Which also made his heart a little lighter. Surely it indicated she felt something for him. He thought they'd been getting closer during their London phone calls, but it all seemed to have disappeared after they'd arrived yesterday.

Oh, she'd played the part of loving wife at the wedding ceremony. But instead of relief that she'd be able to fool his mother and friends, he'd been a little let down that it was all an act.

Sophia rose and put the empty glasses back on the drinks tray and wiped up the few wet spots on the glass-top table. Isabella had her head to one side, watching his wife.

"So, Sophia, how did you meet Luca? He has only been to London once in the past month."

Sophia hesitated, twirling her wedding ring. He hadn't seen her nervous often, but she definitely looked uncomfortable. What the hell was Isabella playing at? She was supposed to help ease Sophia's transition to live in Italy, not make her want to go back to London.

He stepped onto the terrace and moved beside his wife, putting his arm around her waist. Only the stiffness in Sophia's body stopped him from kissing her so fully, Isabella would walk out the door and forget her whole stupid party idea.

"*Basta*, Isabella, enough. Your husband must be wondering where you are." If he thought knowing that Isabella was married would ease Sophia's mind, he was mistaken. His wife pulled out of his arms and straightened the cushions on the chairs.

Isabella's eyes darted between them before she let out an annoying laugh. "You are right. Dante does worry. And, I still have some last-minute things to sort out for tomorrow," she said, rising from her chair. "It is okay that I take your car home, Luca? I will come and pick you up at ten tomorrow morning, Sophia, for our shopping. *Ciao*." She strolled toward the door, not waiting for a response.

Sophia finished straightening the chairs and resumed her seat. She stared at her wine before taking a sip and then gazed toward the gardens, in effect dismissing him.

"I am sorry about that. Isabella doesn't understand the word 'no.' She never has. You can come with me on site visits next weekend," he said, as he sat back in his chair. He wanted to take Sophia's hand, but she pulled it off the armrest as he reached for it.

"It's not the site visit I'm upset about. You expect me to go shopping for a party even you don't want me to attend, with your … your … girlfriend?" Her voice shook and the hand in her lap clenched into a fist.

"Isabella is not my girlfriend, beyond the fact that she is a girl and a friend. We've known each other since school. There is nothing romantic between us. She is married, as am I."

Sophia snorted but didn't make any other reply.

"And who is this Jonathan? Do you expect me to believe that you just happened to meet him on your first day in the country?"

"Yes, I expect you to believe that. Because it's the truth." She stood and crossed her arms over her chest. He searched her face, trying to decide if she was lying.

"And yet you do not believe me when I say the

truth."

"I guess we're at an impasse then. I'm hot and dusty from my walk. I'm going to wash up before dinner. Are we eating again at eight?"

"Yes."

She strode back into the house, not looking back.

He let out a sigh. This wasn't how today was supposed to have gone. He was supposed to come home, find Sophia waiting, happy to see him. He'd planned for them to stroll through the village, maybe have an aperitif in the bar by the piazza. Then a walk home, eat an enjoyable meal together, and hopefully, maybe, a kiss or two to make a start on the physical side of their relationship. Instead, he'd come home to find she'd disappeared, then she'd shown up in the truck of a foreign man who she claimed had rescued her. Rescuing her was his job. He was the husband. Had he failed her already?

When Isabella had called to remind him of the party, he'd told her he couldn't come now because he was married. She'd gone mental on him, racing over to his office and berating him in person for abandoning his bride in a foreign country where she didn't speak the language. Isabella had then insisted they go to the villa immediately so she could meet Sophia. He never expected her to pull some power play, though. He'd have a word with her tomorrow. Isabella was his oldest friend who had made school life bearable. But he wouldn't let her cause a misunderstanding between him and Sophia.

On the other hand, a party would inevitably mean he got to hold his wife in his arms, maybe even kiss her.

It didn't have to be such a disaster. He rubbed his hands together. Yes, this may work out after all.

Chapter Six

Sophia paced the hallway, listening to the clock in the front room tick away the minutes like a countdown to destruction. She jumped at the sound of Maria banging a pot in the kitchen. Despite being tired from her long walk yesterday, her mind had kept replaying the argument with Luca on the terrace, leaving her unable to sleep.

He was right. She had nothing to base her accusations on except her own insecurities. Today she'd discover if Luca and Isabella were lovers. And if they were, she'd be back on a plane before he could say the word "annulment." There was a painful twinge in her chest, but she ignored it. Better to end the whole charade now before she got too used to this life. Too involved with Luca.

The roar of the Maserati's engine in the drive alerted her to the arrival of Isabella for their "shopping" trip. She was pretty sure "shopping" was euphemistic in this case for "interrogation." Well, she had some questions of her own to ask. She picked up her bag from the entryway table and stepped out into the spring sunshine.

Isabella slid out of the low-slung sports car with a grace and elegance Sophia could only dream of achieving. The beautiful woman wore a white dress that buttoned down the front and a pair of black stilettoes.

Sophia glanced down at her navy-blue skirt, aqua top and ballerina flats, and her throat tightened. Maybe she should just go straight to the airport now.

"*Ciao*, Sophia. I am pleased you are ready to go. We have a lot to do. Luca has already left?" She glanced to where the Land Rover was usually parked.

"Yes, he went hours ago. But he left me money and credit cards and a note to spend as much as I wanted." She omitted the part about waiting in her room until she heard the front door close behind Luca to avoid a repeat of last night's uncomfortably silent meal.

"*Buono*. I will give you the Maserati keys. My husband does not let me have a sports car. He thinks I will kill myself. So I have to steal Luca's when I have the chance. Ah, here is my driver now." A white Mercedes pulled into the drive, complete with uniformed chauffeur.

The driver jumped out and opened the doors for them. Sophia clambered in beside Isabella and took a deep breath.

"So, you think Luca and I are lovers," Isabella said, before Sophia could even exhale.

"Did Luca tell you that's what I thought?" Was nothing private in her marriage?

"He did not need to. I saw it in your face when you arrived home yesterday. You did not like it when I put my arm through his. And Luca did not like when you came home with another man."

"No."

"Let me ease your heart. Luca and I are friends, nothing more. We are not, and never have been, lovers.

I am in love with my husband. When you meet him tonight, you will know. I am sorry for yesterday. I was rude on purpose. I wanted to see what you would do."

"Did I pass your test?"

"Yes, with, how do you say, flying the colors?"

"Flying colors. But I don't understand."

"When Luca told me yesterday that he was married, I worried. He had not told me of any woman he was seeing, and I thought maybe you had tricked him into marriage. By pretending to be more than a friend, I wanted to see how you would react. If you were indifferent, then I would know that you did not care for Luca. If you had a fight right there, I would know you did not know him at all. Luca hates airing the dirty clothes in public."

"We had a row after you left."

"Good."

Sophia examined the woman next to her. She couldn't understand Isabella. Was she trying to help? "Good?"

"Oh, yes. Luca needs to be shaken. He has been in control for so long, he does not know how to react when things do not go his way. You need to keep him tipping over."

"I think you mean off-balance."

"Yes, that is it. And so to off-balance him, we are going to find a dress for you to wear tonight that will make him crazy."

"Are you sure you're Luca's friend?"

Isabella's rich laugh filled the car. "Yes, and I want to be your friend, too. So we must make sure you stay together. Marriage is not easy when the man always wants to be in charge. But it can be done."

Four hours later, Sophia stood in front of a full-length mirror in an exclusive boutique and tugged on the hem of the dress she wore. Although dress was a generous word for what was, in effect, just a large, tight shirt. "I can't wear this," she protested.

Isabella cocked her head to one side, her perfectly manicured nail tapping on her crimson-stained lower lip. "No, it is not quite right. But we are getting closer." She turned to the shop assistant and spoke in rapid Italian.

As far as Sophia could tell, they weren't getting any closer. She'd tried on at least twenty dresses, some too long, some too short, some too revealing, others not revealing enough, according to Isabella. Whatever her new friend had in mind, she wasn't going to settle until she found it. This was the third boutique they'd visited. At each, Isabella had been treated like royalty. Shopping was so much nicer when the clothes came to you.

"Ah, this one may work," she declared as Sophia shimmied out of the last outfit. Another dress appeared over the door of the change room, although change palace may be a more apt word. No tiny fitting cubicles in this shop. There was even a sofa and mini fridge full of refreshments.

Sophia hung the dress on the hook behind the door and stared at it. She didn't dare look at the price tag, sure it would make her hyperventilate. Carefully she removed the garment and tried it on. If this didn't tip Luca over, nothing would.

"*Perfetto*," Isabella declared when Sophia emerged

wearing the dress. "Luca will not know what hit him."

• • •

Luca shifted his weight and adjusted his tie, again. With one ear he listened to Stefano, his lawyer friend, with the other he waited for the sound of Sophia's footsteps on the stairs. Isabella had insisted that Sophia make an entrance, but he didn't appreciate being kept in the dark. She was his wife, damn it; he had a right to see her first.

Isabella had called him late in the afternoon to say that their shopping trip had taken longer than expected. So Sophia was going to get ready at Isabella's place and they'd see him there. When he'd asked to speak with his wife, she'd laughed and asked if he thought she'd kidnapped her. But after the tight-lipped silence he'd endured through dinner the previous night, he'd wanted to make sure Sophia was happy with that arrangement and hadn't been coerced by Isabella's forceful personality. Sophia had assured him that she'd had a great day and would see him later. As she'd handed the phone back to Isabella, Luca could have sworn he heard his wife giggle.

He'd rushed to get ready and was the first to arrive. Instead of being able to see his bride, however, Isabella had insisted that Sophia be left alone to rest.

Enough was enough. He wanted his wife at his side. This was, after all, why he married her. The little voice in his head laughed, but then went silent as a noise at the top of the stairs drew all eyes upward.

Luca's heart fibrillated for a moment before racing.

His mouth went dry and he pulled at his tie again, trying to get more air into his lungs. Sophia glided down the stairs, stopping halfway. Even from a distance he could see how the green of her dress brought out the amazing emerald color of her eyes. The gown was a mix of brocade and satin, wrapped around her body like a ribbon. Her delicate shoulders and collarbone were exposed by the strapless dress. And with her long, golden hair pulled up, the graceful column of her neck called out for his kisses. He shifted again, but this time to disguise the growing pressure in his trousers. Sophia looked as though she'd been gift wrapped. The perfect present.

"*Prego*." You are welcome, Isabella murmured by his right shoulder before she ascended the stairs to meet Sophia halfway.

Isabella tapped a spoon against her glass, calling the attention of those few who weren't already staring at Sophia. "Thank you all for coming tonight. I would like to introduce you to my new friend, and Luca's bride, Sophia Castellioni. Sophia is from London, so we all get to practice our English tonight." Isabella's announcement was met with clapping and a chorus of congratulations in a mix of English and Italian. Stefano grabbed his hand to shake it, but Luca couldn't take his eyes from Sophia.

Isabella whispered something into his wife's ear. Sophia smiled and walked down the remaining stairs, stopping on the last one. He rushed over to her and took her hand in his, placing a kiss on the back of it. Because if he kissed her lips, it would take at least four men to pull him away from her.

"You are so beautiful," he managed to say past a lump in his throat.

"*Grazie*," she replied with another of her devastating smiles. She leaned toward him and he inhaled her intoxicating perfume. Her warm breath caressed his ear as she whispered, "Let's party."

• • •

Sophia sipped her prosecco and listened to her husband, his hand resting at the small of her back, discuss the latest political scandal with several other party-goers. Every couple of minutes he'd lean down and ask if she was okay, if she needed anything, or if there was something she wanted to add to the conversation. He was the perfect husband, attentive and caring.

Isabella topped up Sophia's wine glass again, and soon she was clinging to Luca, glad when his arm went around her shoulders and she could lean into his strong body. She glanced at him out of the corner of her eye, still somewhat amazed that she was with him. When she'd come down the stairs, Luca had been the only person she'd noticed. With his black suit, snow-white shirt, and crimson tie, he looked suave and incredibly sexy. Her husband. In name only—for now.

"It is warm in here. Shall we step out onto the terrace?" he whispered in her ear as the lawyer in their group droned on about some legislative fiasco that had recently been reported.

She nodded her consent, and Luca made their

excuses and led her out the patio doors. Potted Lemon trees stood sentinel against the balustrade. Laden with scented blossoms, they glowed from the fairy lights twined in their branches. A bubbling fountain masked the sound of a hundred conversations in the house. They were meters from a crowd but felt alone. Sophia took a deep breath. This was romance. She didn't know why she'd avoided it all her life. It was exquisite, addictive. A shiver swept through her.

"Are you cold?" Before she could respond, Luca peeled off his jacket and wrapped it around her shoulders, then pulled her against him. His heart thudded under her ear, and she couldn't help snuggling further into his embrace, her arms going around his waist so her body was flush against his.

"I'm good," she replied, her voice refusing to rise above a whisper.

"Did you have a fun day? I worried that Isabella would be too controlling, especially when you didn't come home."

"No, we had a great time. I like her. I'm sorry for the things I said last night. I should have believed you."

"*Non è importante*, as long as you are happy now." He pressed a kiss to her forehead.

She was happy.

"Luca, Sophia, some of the guests are leaving and would like to express their well wishes to you before they go." Isabella's voice barely penetrated the haze of bliss.

"We will come in one more minute," Luca replied as if he, too, was reluctant to let go of this moment.

With a sigh she felt as much as heard, Luca led her back into the house for what became an hour of cheek-kissing, hugging, congratulatory good-byes. Finally there was just her, Luca, Isabella, and her husband Dante, left in the entranceway.

Wine glasses that had been abandoned or forgotten littered almost every flat surface. Napkins were tucked into crevices and plates were stacked in the oddest locations. The white hydrangea blossoms that had earlier stood proudly in their glass vases now drooped their heads in exhaustion. Yet a strange energy zipped through Sophia's veins. She didn't want the night to end.

"Come, let us sit in the snug. I think it escaped the worst of the devastation." Isabella led them to a room at the back of the house, off the kitchen. Two comfy-looking sofas were arranged in a V-shape so all could enjoy the view of the moonlight garden through the floor-to-ceiling windows.

Isabella plopped down onto one of the sofas with a loud groan. "Well, I think that was a success," she said. She released the clips at the back of her hair and shook it out.

Dante appeared a moment later, having stopped in the kitchen. He carried a tray with two bottles of wine and four glasses. "Of course it was a success, *tesoro mio*. It did not dare be anything else," Dante replied.

He poured the wine and passed the long-stem glasses around. "This is a special vintage from my grandfather's vineyard. I offer a toast to a long and happy marriage for our friends, Luca and Sophia."

"With lots of babies," Isabella added, holding her

glass in the air.

"*Grazie*," Luca replied, his eyes focused on Sophia's face. He took a sip of the wine, then placed the glass on the coffee table. Sitting back, he put his arm along the back of the sofa, behind her head.

"It was a lovely party, thank you," Sophia said. Luca's arm slid off the sofa and onto her shoulders. His fingers toyed with a loose strand of hair against her nape. Whether it was the wine, or his gentle, hypnotic caress, within five minutes she was snuggled against him, her head on his shoulder.

Opposite her, Isabella had taken off her shoes, and Dante reached down and began to massage her feet. They were an amazing couple. Throughout the day, whenever Isabella had spoken of her husband, her eyes had gone dreamy and a soft smile lifted her lips.

When Sophia had met Dante earlier in the afternoon, she'd been intimidated by the man's size. Isabella had said her husband played rugby for the Italian national team, but he was even larger than she'd imagined. Within ten minutes, however, his gentle manner and ready laugh had put her at ease and all she saw now was a man desperately in love with his wife. Sophia had never seen such blatant affection—was it a rare thing or did she just not know the right kind of people?

The general discussion was about the party. Who looked older or younger, who had broken up or gotten back together. At some point Dante opened the second bottle of wine and refilled her glass. By then Sophia let the conversation flow over her as she cuddled into

Luca's warmth.

She'd just closed her eyes when a loud snore echoed through the room. Sophia sat up, worried the noise had come from her. Looking across at the other sofa, Isabella sat with her head thrown back, her mouth wide open. Dante chuckled before gently pulling his wife into his arms.

"Are you sure you do not want to stay the night? The guest room is all set up," Dante offered.

"No, we had better get home," Luca replied. Sophia had noticed that he'd stopped drinking a couple of hours ago, and his glass of wine that Dante had poured for the toast remained full on the coffee table.

Sophia clambered to her feet, only to find the floor had moved on her. She lurched against Luca. "Oh dear," she murmured.

Luca laughed, then scooped her up in his arms. "Don't worry, I've got you." He carried her to the front of the house, while Dante had Isabella in his arms.

"I wish we had a picture of this. Having to carry our wives after a party," Dante said. "It would get us both out of the doghouse for months to come."

"I wish," Luca joked. "*Buonanotte*, Dante. *Grazie*."

The cool night air refreshed Sophia for a moment. But as soon as Luca put her down to open the car door, she swayed against him.

"I think I'm drunk." She tried to whisper but it came out very loud.

"Yes, I think you are," Luca said from a distance.

She waited while he climbed into the driver's seat and fastened her seatbelt. "I've never been drunk before.

I kinda like it." Everything tingled and all the tension of the past weeks had melted away.

"You may not like it so much tomorrow. I don't suggest you make a habit of it." Luca started the car and soon the reflection of the street lights whizzing over the bonnet of the car made her dizzy, so she closed her eyes.

"Have I disappointed you? I don't want to disappoint you. I disappoint everyone." He'd placed his jacket around her shoulders, and she snuggled into the warmth, inhaling deeply of his citrus-sandalwood aftershave.

"No, you haven't disappointed me. The opposite, in fact. You were amazing tonight. And besides, you're a cute drunk."

"Have you ever been drunk?"

"Not since I was eighteen. I don't like to lose control."

"Me neither. It's not safe. But I feel safe with you."

"Glad to hear it. I will always care for you, Sophia."

"Still, I wonder what it would take to make you lose control."

"At the moment, just one of your smiles." At least that's what she thought he said. It could have been her imagination, because the next thing she knew she woke up near enough naked in her bed.

Chapter Seven

Luca sensed rather than heard Sophia descend the stairs. Through the open dining room door, he saw her cling to the banister. Each step was tentative, and she stopped twice before managing to make her way to the table. He folded his newspaper and placed it beside his plate.

"Tea," she whispered. "Must have tea. Too much evil prosecco. Very bad head."

He poured a cup of tea and placed it in front of her. She sipped it slowly with her eyes closed, allowing him to drink in the sight of her. She'd obviously just dragged herself out of bed and thrown on a pair of jeans and a knit top. Her hair was tousled and hung in loose waves down her back—disheveled and delectable. The now familiar rush of heat flooded his body at her just-woken look.

Last night at the party, she'd held his hand or tucked her body against his, whispered into his ear, and smiled at him like a woman in love. He doubted a single person had left the party not believing theirs was a love match. He'd even been fooled once or twice himself. Sophia was a damn good actress. He needed to learn to tell when she wasn't faking, because he wanted to know the real woman, not the one she put on display for everyone else.

She'd fallen asleep on the drive home, and he'd been unable to wake her when they'd arrived. So he'd carried her to her room and managed to get her into bed. He'd pulled the pins out of her hair so they didn't poke her in the night. The beautiful dress she'd worn didn't look comfortable to sleep in, so he'd eased down the zipper, to discover she was wearing only the tiniest scrap of underpants and no bra. *Grazie a Dio,* he hadn't known that earlier in the evening or it would have driven him insane. As it was, it took every ounce of self-control he had to pull the blankets up over her and go sleep in his cold, lonely bed.

Dio mio, what is wrong with me? They'd been married for three days and already this union was proving anything but convenient. He'd thought he could wed a desirable woman and still pursue the passion of his business. This was exactly why he hadn't wanted to marry for love. He'd seen that fickle emotion turn other men's ambition to dust and had vowed the same wouldn't happen to him.

However, now he was beginning to resent every minute his business took him away from Sophia. It must be the fact that they hadn't consummated their marriage. The sexual tension was distracting him. Once they made love, he'd be able to concentrate on work again. Satisfied that was the answer, he returned to his breakfast.

"I thought you English girls were used to staying up all night and clubbing till dawn?"

"Not this English girl. I'm used to being in bed by eleven with a good book," she admitted, finally opening her eyes. "If you wanted a girl to stay up and party all night, you should have married Olivia."

"No, I married the right girl. I'll promise to have you in bed by eleven if you replace the good book with a good man." He reached across the table and tucked a strand of her hair behind her ear.

"I'll consider your offer," she replied, her voice raspy.

She finished her tea and he poured another cup for her. "Um, I didn't do anything stupid last night, did I?"

"No, you were a perfect angel."

"I'm not sure perfect angels wake up naked." There was no censure in her eyes, just confusion.

"Not generally. But I promise I closed my eyes," he lied. "I didn't think you'd sleep very well in your dress."

"Well, thank you for your help. I didn't want anything to have happened and I missed it."

"I don't take advantage of women who have passed out. And trust me, *amore*, when I make love to you, you will remember it."

"Good to know," she mumbled into her tea.

He bit back the offer to show her right now. "I am afraid I am going to have to leave you again. Every year I take my workers to one of the matches between the Milan football teams, Internazionale and AC Milan. That happens to be today. It is booked months in advance. After the match we go out for something to eat. I should be home by nine or ten." It was usually one of his favorite days of the year, but for the first time he'd rather watch the game on TV if it meant he could be with Sophia.

She stole a piece of toast off his plate, giving him a wink as she did, even though there were several others on the toast rack on the table.

"That's okay. I plan on spending the day sleeping and reading, probably in that order. I don't think I'll be much company anyway." She dropped the purloined toast on her plate after one bite and rubbed her fingers on her temples.

"Speaking of reading, there's a present from your friend Jonathan on my desk—a couple of books on learning Italian. At least the man is practical. He also left a note apologizing for not coming to the party. Evidently a delivery of concrete he was expecting arrived late, and he had to stay behind and supervise the pour."

"That's a shame. Maybe I'll run into him in the village again and can thank him personally. I'm happy to get the books, though. I want to start learning right away so I can understand people. It's very frustrating when you don't know what's going on. All your friends were very nice last night about speaking English when I was near."

Luca bit his tongue. He couldn't demand that she not see the other man. He had to trust she wouldn't betray him or damage his reputation. "You were the star of the night. Everyone loved you."

"Well, they may not love me so much if I'm still speaking only English a year from now. Oh, by the way, Isabella and I arranged to meet in Milan tomorrow. Any chance I can get a ride into the city with you in the morning? What time do you leave?"

"Yes, she mentioned it to me. I usually leave by six thirty. However, tomorrow I'll not go until eight so you don't have to get up so early." At least they'd have the hour's commute into Milan together.

It would have to do … for now.

• • •

Sophia flipped through the fabric samples, trying to find the perfect one to go with the sofa she'd seen in the village her first day. Isabella was going to help arrange the purchase and reupholster work. It was ideal for the front sitting room. After she got rid of the red monstrosity, that was.

"Who decorated Luca's villa?" Because if they were a professional, they should be reported to whoever certified interior designers in Italy.

"Oh, some woman he was dating at the time. She had ideas of being Signora Castellioni. Luca was too busy to supervise the design himself, so just gave her the money to do it. The furniture is atrocious, is it not? I think she just went into the shop and asked for the most expensive items." Isabella flipped through the wallpaper samples, occasionally checking a pattern against a photo she held.

"What happened to her? I mean why did they break up?"

"I did not get the full story. But I heard she was baking two cakes at the same time."

Sophia widened her eyes and waiting for the explanation. Isabella's expressions were often a mix-up of English and literally translated Italian idioms.

"She was also seeing some other man. He proposed first, so she went with him. I do not think Luca was too upset, except when the furniture started to arrive."

"Has Luca dated many women?"

"No, he has been too busy at work. Being successful has always been his obsession. I think it comes from when he was at school."

"Yes, Luca said you were at school together. Did something happen there that made him so determined?"

"It was not one thing. You see, Luca he came from a, what do you call, regular family. His parents were not rich, but they were not poor either. But his father, he wanted Luca to go to private school so he could get a good education and be important. However, some of the other children did not like that people without lots of money were going to their school. So they made it very hard, always picking on Luca, telling him he was not good enough. I think it made him more determined to be a success, so he could show them."

"What about your family?"

"My family were very rich. But I liked Luca. He was not up himself, as you English say. I could talk to him. My parents, they had lots of money but no love. They only cared that I did not get into trouble, darken the family name. That is probably why I married the first man who said he loved me."

"Dante?"

"No, I was married once, before Dante. To a terrible man. He hit me and stole all my money. Luca was very angry. He tried to warn me Federico was no good, but I would not listen. Your husband, he is very protective of the people he cares for. But you will know this already, because he loves you."

Should she tell Isabella that theirs was a business arrangement? No, she'd let Isabella keep her delusions. Then maybe Sophia could indulge in them from time to time. It may be the only thing to cling to in the lonely months ahead, left in the villa with two people she could barely communicate with.

"Isabella, do you have any interest in interior design?"

"Yes, of course. But I have no experience. I was a journalist until a few months ago. It was very stressful, and Dante and I want to have a baby. Stress is not good for the conception."

"Would you be interested in working with me? I've almost completed my interior design course and was thinking about starting a business." Her coursework had been slow, with little time to devote to it in London. But with all the time she currently had on her hands, she could probably finish within a month. Then she'd be well and truly bored.

"It sounds a very interesting idea. I will discuss it with Dante. What does Luca say about you starting a business? He has lots of money; I am sure he does not expect his wife to work."

"He's so busy, I'm sure he won't mind." She turned her attention back to the swatches. "What do you think of this fabric?"

After choosing a suitable material, they went for lunch and then a pedicure. Sophia tried to be discreet in checking the time, but Isabella caught her.

"Am I boring you?"

"No, not at all. Why would you say that?" Sophia

stalled.

"Because you keep looking at your watch. If I am not boring, then you must be counting the minutes until you see Luca again."

Busted.

"Do not worry. I did the same when I started to see Dante. And even now, when he is away playing rugby and I cannot go with him, I feel like a piece of me is missing. It is stupid, no? We are smart, beautiful women. But without our man, we are a little lost. Some days it makes me sad to be so dependent. But then I look at my husband and I would not have my life different. I love him and do not care that his happiness is more important than my own. Because I know he feels the same way."

Sophia looked away. Would she and Luca ever feel that way about each other? Did she want to be so dependent on someone for happiness? No, it would be better if she built her own life, found her own place in the world. Then if Luca tired of her, she would have something to fall back on. It was too dangerous to put all her eggs in the Luca basket—no matter how enticing he made it seem.

Two hours later, Sophia was giving herself the same pep talk. She sat beside her husband in the Maserati, crawling through Milan traffic. Luca seemed deep in thought as he stared out the windscreen, his hands clenched on the steering wheel.

"Is everything okay?"

He turned to her as if surprised she was there. "Sorry, my mind was still at work."

"Is there a problem? Sometimes talking about it

helps."

"No, I can take care of it. Tell me about your shopping with Isabella. Do you need more money?"

His message was loud and clear—she was his wife, his partner, only when other people were around.

• • •

Sophia put her book down on the table, rested her head on the back of the sofa, and stared at the ceiling. *This isn't working. None of it.*

Marriage to Luca was supposed to have given her financial security, time to pursue her dreams, and become the person she wanted to be, far from the troubled girl who had fled her home at the age of sixteen. Instead she was a twenty-three-year-old woman who spent her whole day in anxious anticipation of the fifteen minutes or so when she saw her husband—if she saw him.

After three weeks of living in the villa, she knew if she got up at 6:00 a.m., she just might catch Luca before he left for work. He'd ask her what she planned to do that day, his hot gaze roving over her body. But then he'd politely kiss her goodbye on the cheek, and the next sound was his car fading into the distance. Maybe if she moved into his room, he'd find more time for her. But he still treated her like a possession, albeit a pampered one. She was the rare pet he'd bought to show off to his friends but forgot when it suited him.

Before she could share her body with him, she needed him to share some small part of his life with her.

Preferably a non-business part, if that even existed.

Sometimes she even stayed up until he came home around midnight. He'd look exhausted, dark shadows under his eyes, his jaw covered in stubble. Again he'd ask about her day and respond with a list of meetings or contracts he'd bid for when she asked about his. With the amount of work he seemed to accomplish each day, she wasn't surprised he was so tired.

So far, Sophia had divided her day between her interior design coursework and learning Italian from the books that Jonathan had given her. She practiced her pronunciation on Vittore and Maria. She'd also discovered a love of gardening and spent many hours following the older man around as he explained to her, patiently and slowly, about the plants he tended. She had a grubby little notebook she carried with her, and when he used a word she didn't understand, she wrote it down to look up later.

Every couple of days, Luca would email a letter or document for her to check his English. It took a whole twenty minutes to correct and return each one, so they neither filled her time nor brought her any closer to her husband.

Last week, when the weather had turned wet, Sophia had asked Maria to teach her to cook, and she'd spent several happy days in the kitchen. She could now manage to make a couple of Italian specialties. While showing her how to prepare ravioli so they didn't explode while cooking, Maria had prattled on about *bambini*. With the pointed look Maria had given her during the conversation, the cook probably wondered if there would ever be any children in the house.

With a sigh, Sophia got up from her chair and moved to the mantel, running her index finger over Luca's handsome face in the photo with his mother. If she was unhappy with her marriage, then it was time she did something about it and stopped being a doormat. What would Luca would do if, when he came home tonight, he found a note saying she'd gone to Paris for the weekend? Would he worry? Call her back immediately? Or not even notice she was gone? The phone rang and she raced to answer it.

"*Amore*, I will be working very late and I have a breakfast meeting in the morning, so I will be staying at the flat in Milan tonight," Luca said. "Sleep well, and I will see you tomorrow."

After hanging up, she released a loud moan of frustration, glad there was no one else in the house to hear her. Nope, this marriage wasn't working. The question was, what was she going to do about it?

• • •

Sophia paid for the get-well-soon card and stamps and sat down at the village café to write a note to her mother so she could post it right away. James had called earlier in the week to say their mother hadn't responded well to an initial cancer treatment, so the doctors were trying something else. It seemed pathetic to write a card to her own mother. A real daughter, a good daughter, would hop on a plane and go visit her. But she wasn't ready yet—doubted she'd ever be—to see her parents again.

Their lack of love and support had destroyed any connection she'd had with them as a child. So when Kathy Summers had attacked her, Sophia hadn't turned to her parents. She'd left home and never looked back.

"Sophia, do you need rescuing again?"

She shielded her eyes from the hot sun to see Jonathan standing in front of her.

"No, I'm fine today. Sorry about last time. It was all rather awkward, wasn't it? I'm glad to see you again, though. I wanted to thank you for the learn-to-speak-Italian books. They've been a great help."

The waitress chose that moment to ask what she wanted, and she ordered an iced coffee and biscotti in Italian.

"You have improved," Jonathan said, laughter in his eyes.

"*Grazie*, would you like to join me? It would be nice to speak English with someone for a few minutes."

"If you think your husband won't mind," he answered but pulled out a chair anyway.

"My husband doesn't control who I speak with."

Jonathan placed his order with the hovering waitress, who Sophia guessed was trying to decipher their conversation. Teresa, the cleaner girl, walked by and called out a greeting.

"You're like a local," Jonathan said as another couple waved to her.

"I've ordered a few pieces of furniture and bought some other things from the village, so I guess people know who I am now."

"Do you know much about furniture and stuff?"

Jonathan took a sip of his iced coffee.

"Yes. I've just sent in my last assignment on my course. Provided I pass, I will be a certified interior designer. Of course, it's a British certification, so I'm not sure how it will translate here in Italy."

"Would you be interested in taking on a client? I don't care where your certificate comes from. I have no idea how to decorate and furnish my place. Bricks and plaster I can understand. But all those frilly bits scare me."

"Frilly bits are what makes a house a home. You need to get in touch with your feminine side."

"My feminine side walked out the door two years ago. And good riddance to her. What I need is someone else's feminine side to guide me."

She searched his face. "Are you serious? You want to hire me?"

"Absolutely."

"But I barely speak Italian and don't drive. My friend Isabella is thinking of helping me, but she's busy for the next two weeks. She's travelling with her husband on an international rugby tournament."

"You and Isabella are friends now?"

"Yes, it was all a misunderstanding."

"Glad to hear it. Speaking of misunderstandings, your husband is a pretty powerful bloke around here. One word from him and I'll never get another delivery of concrete or anyone to work for me. He's not going to mind if you help me out?"

"Oh no, Luca doesn't care what I get up to during the day. As long as I'm available when he needs me to attend a business dinner, the rest of my time is my own."

Jonathan looked skeptical but shrugged. "Brilliant. I can drive wherever we need to go. As long as you don't mind my old truck. How soon can you start?"

"Right away. I just need to finish my letter and post it, then I'm all yours."

The waitress dropped a cup at the next table before scurrying back inside the café.

"Wonder what flustered her?" Jonathan remarked.

"I don't know. Something I said?"

She glanced back into the café to see all the patrons staring at her. Very odd.

Chapter Eight

Luca put his feet up on the desk in his study, leaned back in the chair, and closed his eyes. *Dio*, he was tired. Everything took so much longer since his marriage. He had to read everything multiple times, focus twice as hard. If he didn't, Sophia's face would appear on the page in front of him and scatter his concentration.

He'd tried staying away from the villa, hoping that not seeing his wife in person would lessen her influence. Yet each night he returned home, he felt her presence. Staying at his flat in Milan had also been a disaster, leaving him unable to sleep knowing Sophia was so far away.

When they did spend time together, she would fidget and tidy things, move about the room as if trying to keep her distance from him. How could he make love to her if she could barely stand to be near him?

He'd been living in purgatory for over three weeks. Something had to give. And soon.

His eyes snapped open at a faint noise. He blinked, sure he had fallen asleep and was dreaming. Sophia stood in front of him, wearing only a lace-trimmed ivory camisole and silky shorts. Her hair was tousled and her face scrubbed clean of makeup. He'd never seen her more beautiful.

"I didn't hear you come home," her voice was

barely above a whisper, as if she was afraid to shatter the moment with words. "I came down to get water, lots of water. Vittore introduced me to *limoncello* and kept refilling my glass. I saw the light on in here..." The words tumbled out of her mouth, and she kept staring at his throat. "You look tired," she said almost to herself.

Before he could respond, she moved behind his chair and started to massage his temples. He released the breath he hadn't even been aware he was holding with a groan of pleasure. Her touch, tentative at first, became bolder as he relaxed.

"I have been working on a presentation for Chet Wilkins. There's an abandoned village for sale a couple hours out of Teramo. If he buys it for his hotel, and I get the contract for the renovations, then my company is guaranteed work for several years. In this economy, that's crucial," he said. He wanted her to understand it was work that was keeping him from her, not a lack of interest.

Her fingers ventured into his hair, massaging his scalp. He should tell Sophia to stop; her small hands were working wonders on reducing his tension level—but they were raising other parts of him.

"I'd like to know more. What you do fascinates me. I can't imagine bringing a whole village back to life," she prompted.

"Really?" Even his mother's eyes had glazed over when he'd talked about his work. So he'd learned to not mention it with those outside the business so he didn't bore them.

"Yes. You rebuild parts of the past so future

generations can enjoy them as well."

Sophia seemed genuinely interested. And he longed to let her into this part of his life, to draw closer to her, like a real married couple. Isabella had hated rugby when she'd met Dante. Now she followed him around the world and watched every game. Maybe if Sophia developed an appreciation of architectural restoration, she'd find him more interesting. Then she wouldn't have to pretend so much when they were with others.

"The village I want to show Chet has been abandoned for thirty years. All of the buildings are derelict, but the location is fantastic. It is surrounded by hills and the beautiful Adriatic coast is only a few miles away. It would make a perfect spa hotel, a luxury property where guests could have their own house for privacy."

"It sounds wonderful. But where is Teramo? I don't recognize the name."

"It is almost six hours from here. But there is not so much work in this area now, and I have people relying on me for employment. I can weather a few lean years, but if work is available I cannot, in good faith, turn it down."

Her fingers stilled on his neck. Before she could pull away, he reached for her hands and drew her around in front of him. "What is wrong? Are you worried we will not have enough money?" Would she leave him if he lost the company? The tension she'd released with her massage came back twice as hard in his stomach.

"No, I've lived with nothing before. I can do it again. It's…"

"Tell me, Sophia. I'm your husband. You can share your worries with me." She squeezed his hands lightly but didn't pull away. A lock of her hair slipped from behind her shoulder and caressed her face. He wanted to tuck it back behind her ear, but his hand refused to let go of hers.

"It's just that I barely see you now. If you take this job, I won't see you at all." There was a catch in her voice as she said the last words. His chest constricted, and he drew in a large breath to ease the tightness. Money didn't matter to her, she wanted him.

He stood and pulled her into his arms, resting his chin at the top of her head. She didn't resist or stiffen, and he reveled in her scent, the feel of her in his arms. "We'll work something out. I wouldn't leave you."

"I miss you, Luca." She whispered the words and a lump formed in his throat. He'd brought her to his country and then virtually abandoned her. And she hadn't once complained or demanded that he stay home. He was a terrible husband.

She raised her face and he searched her eyes. The fake smile he'd come to loathe was gone. "I miss you, too. We must fix this mistake. We haven't had a honeymoon. Why don't we go away this weekend?" He held his breath, waiting for her answer.

Her eyes sparkled. "Sounds wonderful."

• • •

Sophia had three days to get over herself—stop wanting what she couldn't get and hold onto what she had. Luca was taking her up to romantic Lake Como on Friday night, and she'd be damned if she was coming back a virgin. She'd let the past control enough of her life. If she was going to move forward in her marriage, then she needed to get out of the yellow bedroom and into Luca's.

She pulled off her muddy gloves and wiped the sweat off her forehead with her arm. It was almost ten o'clock, and the sun had started to burn her fair skin. Vittore had allocated a small patch of the garden to her so she could try various flower combinations. The formal Italian garden, with its topiary and manicured lawns, was beautiful. But she wanted a tiny spot of wild abandon where flowers could grow free of borders and boundaries—able to touch each other in the gentle breeze, support each other in a fierce wind.

Her mobile phone rang in her gardening bag, and she quickly dug it out. She didn't get many calls. Isabella was still away with Dante at a rugby tournament and Olivia was at a modeling assignment in the Caribbean. She'd already spoken to her brother James yesterday, so that eliminated all the usual callers. Maybe Jonathan was calling to change their appointment to go antique hunting in Bergamo.

When she finally extricated her phone, the caller display said "Luca Office."

"Hello?" Hopefully he'd ascribe the breathlessness of her voice to some physical activity. He'd come home late last night, long after she'd gone to bed. And she'd slept in this morning. So she hadn't seen him since the encounter in his office two nights ago. If he was cancelling their honeymoon, maybe she would join

Isabella at Dante's tournament in Ireland.

"Sophia, you must move your things into my bedroom. Quickly, before dinner."

"Umm, why?" They'd been married a month and now he suddenly was demanding that she sleep with him? Her independent hackles rose while her lower body tingled.

"My mother has found out about our marriage, and she is flying in this afternoon. I have to pick her up from the airport at four o'clock. Chiara, my secretary, is away and the temporary secretary has only now given me the message." There was a slight panic in his voice.

"And you don't want your mother to know you're not sleeping with your wife?"

"Please, Sophia. You don't understand about Italian mothers. They are insane. Especially when they have only one son. We can pretend we are in love, like we did at the party."

She'd woken up naked the next day then, too. Her three days had become six hours.

"I take it you'll be home for dinner, then."

"Yes. See you later, *amore*. And, Sophia, we will not do anything you don't want. Okay?"

The question wasn't what she wanted to do but whether she had the guts to do it. In the meantime, however, she had to get ready for her mother-in-law's inspection.

She hurried to find Maria and alert her to the extra guest for dinner. Usually, Sophia ate with Maria and Vittore in the kitchen when Luca wasn't home, which was most nights. Tonight, however, they'd eat in the dining room. Then she had to find Teresa, the cleaning girl from the village, and instruct her to get her bedroom ready while she moved her things into Luca's room. Sophia ignored the shaking in her hands and raced toward the house.

She took a deep breath and opened the door to Luca's bedroom, their bedroom. Teresa was still downstairs, washing the entryway floor, so Sophia went over to make the massive, king-sized bed. The crisp, white sheets had been tossed back, and she imagined Luca throwing them off before rolling out of bed. Did he wear pajamas? She looked around but couldn't see any. Did he sleep naked? The tingling in her belly started all over again.

She held Luca's pillow against her face for a moment to breathe in the sandalwood scent he wore. As she smoothed the sheets, she bit her lip at the possibility of wrinkling them tonight. Her heart raced and the tingling spread downward to the back of her thighs.

With a last caress of the pillowcase, she turned away from the bed and the unnerving thoughts associated with it. A large walk-in wardrobe led off a hallway to the left. Luca's clothes were neatly arranged to one side; however, there was plenty of room left for her few belongings. The small hallway opened up to a massive bathroom with a large marble tiled shower, claw-foot tub and twin sinks. The suite was very masculine and seemed to be one of the few areas of the house that reflected Luca's taste. Thankfully, the ex-girlfriend hadn't picked out the furniture for this room.

After moving her things, she instructed Teresa to get

the yellow bedroom ready for guests. It was the nicest one in the house, apart from the master, and she was sure Luca's mother was used to sleeping there when visiting. To keep her mind off her mother-in-law's imminent arrival, she spent the rest of the day in the kitchen, helping Maria prepare the meal, which would be as elaborate as the one served on her first night at the villa.

Hours later, Sophia stood in front of the full-length mirror in the bathroom. She had no idea what to wear to meet her mother-in-law, finally deciding to go for a soft, blue-gray knit dress, one she'd bought during a shopping spree with Isabella. She hoped it said elegant and confident, neither of which she was feeling at the moment. Maria had assured her that Luca's mother was a kind woman. However, Sophia wasn't too sure how she would react to meeting Luca's *fatto compiuto* bride.

Ready early, she tried to read but couldn't concentrate on the words. When she heard the unmistakable growl of the Maserati's engine, she moved into the front hallway where she fiddled with the flowers in the vase on the table.

The door swung open and a tall, stylish woman with short, black hair swept in. A light gray trouser suit emphasized her lean form. Once again, Sophia was out-classed. Dark brown eyes surveyed her, as one would a strange dog to ascertain whether it was friendly or not.

"Mamma, this is Sophia," Luca said, coming to stand beside his wife, his hand on her lower back. "Sophia, this is my mother, Giada Tellier."

The Italian greeting she'd practiced all afternoon shriveled on her tongue. "I am pleased to meet you,"

Sophia ventured in English. A faint pressure from Luca's hand at her back propelled her forward, and she hugged her mother-in-law as she'd seen most Italians do when they greeted family or friends. "You must be exhausted from your trip. Would you like to freshen up before dinner, Signora Tellier?"

"You must call me Giada, or Mamma," the older woman replied. "And, yes, I would like to wash. I am in the yellow bedroom to the right, yes?" she said, already ascending the stairs. "Luca please bring up my bags—after you have properly greeted your wife, of course," she added as Luca took Sophia into his arms.

Luca kissed Sophia, his lips gentle and coaxing. But as soon as his mother's door closed, he pulled back. His affections really were all for show. But that didn't stop her body from reacting to him. At least she didn't have to fake that part. Would it be enough for tonight?

"You are very beautiful, Sophia."

She gave him a hesitant smile and stepped out of his arms. "I'd better go check on dinner." She needed a few minutes, and perhaps a glass of Vittore's *limoncello*, to help her get through the next couple of hours. She didn't think Giada would be as easy to fool as the guests at Isabella's party.

She tasted the soup and asked Maria if they should add a little more spice. She'd noticed during the few meals she'd shared with Luca that he always added a few dashes of pepper sauce to the soup.

Vittore laughed and responded with a comment she took to mean she was taking over as teacher. But Maria put an extra two shakes of hot sauce into the pan, then tried it again herself. The cook was nodding her approval when her eyes darted behind Sophia, toward the door.

"I didn't know you spoke Italian so well," Luca said.

"I've been practicing on Maria and Vittore. They are very patient."

Maria broke into a flurry of Italian, and Sophia only managed to catch the odd word. She took the gist to mean that she was too nicely dressed to be standing at the stove and she should sit down and visit with her new mamma.

As she walked toward the door, Luca's eyes roved over her body, and she saw him swallow. Perhaps it wasn't all for show.

In the sitting room, Sophia perched on the edge of the useless red sofa. The new one should be coming in a few days, and she could hardly wait. Luca hadn't commented on any of the other little changes she'd made. But the few personal touches she'd added made the house seem warmer, more homely. At least to her.

Luca poured her a glass of wine and mixed a martini for himself. "I found out how Mamma heard of our marriage," he began.

"Oh, how?"

"You ordered a sofa to be reupholstered. The man who runs the upholstery shop is married to one of Mamma's friends. She got in touch with Mamma on Facebook and asked why she didn't visit when she came back for our wedding."

"Oh, dear. What did your mother say to you?"

"I wouldn't repeat it. But don't fear. I took all the

blame."

"I didn't know about the upholsterer's wife. I was trying to support the local businesses."

"You will soon learn that nothing is secret in a small village. For example, I know you've been meeting with that Englishman, Jonathan." The cold chill that initially swept through Sophia was replaced with a white-hot heat.

"I've done nothing wrong. I'm helping him with the interior design of his house."

"I don't doubt you, *amore*. I only caution. I told you that my reputation is very important to me. I will not accept it for my wife to be talked about visiting another man's house." His accent became more pronounced and his hand clenched at his side.

"And I will not be told who I'm allowed to hang out with. Jonathan is a friend and a client. If you really wanted to stop rumors of me with another man, then perhaps you should be home more often."

Luca put his glass down with a *thunk*. Some of his martini splashed onto his hand. Before she could offer to get a towel to wipe it, he strode across the room and pulled her into his arms.

"*Sì*, perhaps I should come home more often." His head descended and he took her lips in a blistering kiss. Gone was the gentleness of half an hour ago. This was raw passion, demanding she surrender or challenge in return. Not one to back down, she slipped her tongue into his mouth, dueling with his. One of her hands roved over his back, the other tangled into his hair.

As suddenly as he'd pulled her to him, he released

her. Through her heavy breathing, she barely discerned his mother's light footsteps on the marble floor. Luca walked over to the window, his back to her. Her heart pounded, and she ran a shaky hand over her hair.

"Please excuse me, Giada. I just need to ... get something," she said as her mother-in-law entered the room.

"Luca, *cosa c'è?*" Giada asked as Sophia left.

What's up? Sophia'd like to know the answer to that as well.

• • •

Luca rolled the tumbler full of ice and whiskey across his forehead. Well, he'd screwed that up epically. Ask the wife, who can scarcely bear to be in the same room as you—the one you are so desperate to make love to you can't think straight—to move into your bedroom in order to fool your mother that you married for love, then pick a fight with that wife before dinner about something entirely not her fault. Oh yeah, then kiss her until you're about to burst into flames seconds before your mother walks into the room. Smooth, real smooth.

He took a swig of the whiskey. What the hell should he do now? Sophia had hardly spoken a word during dinner and had only picked at her food. His mother had glared at him from soup to tiramisu. He was a failure as both husband and son. He could skulk back to the office or to his flat in Milan. Or he could man up and apologize to his wife. Then sleep on the floor.

He downed the rest of his drink and headed up the

stairs. The bedroom was in darkness when he entered. Perhaps Sophia wasn't even in there. Maybe she'd slipped into one of the other rooms after his mother had gone up to hers. He released a sigh of relief when he heard a soft rustling in the bed.

"I'm not asleep if you want to turn the light on," she whispered.

"The moon is full tonight. I'll open the curtain instead. The light will not be as harsh," he replied. He pressed a button, and the little whirling motor pulled the drapes open. The moonlight bathed the room in an eerie, white light, and he could see Sophia sat up in the bed, the blankets clutched to her chest.

"I have come to apologize. I was a brute." His practiced speech went out the window when he saw her in his bed. He so wanted to climb in beside her, hold her in his arms, and beg her forgiveness that he didn't even know where to start now.

"Luca, you need to know something about me. I've never had to justify my actions to anyone. My parents didn't care what I did. So when you tell me what I can and can't do, I immediately get irritated."

"I understand. But you also need to see how your actions affect my reputation. Remember, the culture is different here. Old-fashioned attitudes still prevail. When a married woman spends time with a man who is not her husband, people will talk. Especially if they are seen leaving together and driving to his house."

"But his house is full of workers. We've never been alone. I don't hang out with Jonathan to start rumors. It never even crossed my mind that people would think I was having an affair with him. We're friends, that's all. Like you and Isabella are friends. I've been alone in this house for weeks. I rarely see you. I feel more like a pampered pet than a wife. Maria and Vittore are nice, but every conversation is a struggle for me. Isabella has been kind and taken me shopping. But she has her own life and travels with Dante as much as she can. I'm bored and lonely. The documents I help you with take only minutes to do. Is it any wonder I've become friends with Jonathan? We speak the same language and he values my advice. He makes me feel needed."

He searched her eyes, wishing he'd turned on the light so he could see her better. It still stung that she gave her friendship so easily to another man when she was so distant with him. "I need you, too, Sophia. And I trust you. I won't mention it again. But I ask that you take care how you act toward him in public."

"I can agree to that."

"And I'm sorry you are lonely. I told you when I proposed that I was very busy with my work. I haven't abandoned you on purpose."

"I know, Luca. I understand that your work is very important to you. And as your wife, if something is important to you, it's important to me. Talk to me about it. Don't shut me out. We have to share things if this marriage is going to work."

"I will try. But you will have to remind me. Sharing is new to me."

"Me too. I've been independent for a long time. I have to make adjustments as well, take your feelings into consideration when I do things. And while we are on the subject of sharing…" She moved to her knees and cupped his face with both hands. He sucked in a breath as her head descended toward his. She'd never initiated a kiss before, and he steeled himself to be gentle, not frighten her with his passion.

Her lips caressed his lightly. One of her hands slipped from his cheek to the back of his head, threading her fingers through his hair. His blood rushed to his groin again and before the last vestige of reason left his brain he released her lips, burying his face in her neck. Her heavy breathing echoed his.

"What else is it you want to share, *carissima mia*?"

"I think it's time we shared your bed on a permanent basis."

Chapter Nine

Sophia took a deep breath. She was finally going to do it. She had a fluttery feeling in her stomach, but no dread.

"Are you sure? I don't want to force you into something you're not ready for," Luca said, but he was already unbuttoning his shirt.

"I'm ready. But before we start, you should know that I have scars. They're not pretty." She searched his eyes for a hint of revulsion, but the light was too dim.

"Are they from your past?" He picked up her hand and pressed a kiss to her inner wrist, setting off a series of tingles up her whole arm.

"Yes."

"Then you are a true ninja, my warrior woman. Your strength and courage draw me to you, Sophia, not push me away."

"If I were a true ninja, I wouldn't have the scars."

"Perhaps. One day, will you trust me enough to share your past with me?"

"I hope so."

"I do as well. Until then, know this, *amore*. We are a team now—partners in good and bad."

She didn't want to mar this moment with her ugly history. The present was far too consuming. Heat radiated off Luca, his scent enveloping her.

"Well, partner, I'm no expert in this, but I think

we've done enough talking. It's time for action." She knelt again on the bed in front of him and spread his unbuttoned shirt wide, roaming her hands over his lightly-haired chest. His muscles quivered under her hands, and he sucked in a quick breath. She reached for his belt and tried to ease the leather through the buckle.

"Whoa, slow down," he said hoarsely, as if he managed to pull just enough air into his lungs to get the words out.

"Don't you like?" She looked up at him, confused.

"I like too much," he reassured her. "But this is your first time—our first time. I don't want to rush anything. Trust me, slower is better … sometimes."

"Well, can I do this?" she breathed against his chest, her tongue flicking his nipples. A sense of power flooded through her as his heart raced beneath her cheek.

His sudden intake of breath brought a smile to her lips. It was replaced however by her own quickly indrawn breath as he ran his thumb over her nipple. "Two can play at that game," he whispered into her ear. "And I know more moves than you." His hands caressed her breasts through the satiny fabric of her camisole top. Her nipples went rigid, and she resented the tiny barrier between his hand and her skin.

"I may be a virgin, but I'm well read," she challenged, eliciting a loud groan from him when her fingers brushed against his erection.

He stood and pulled his clothes off, then looked into her eyes. At her nod, he carefully pulled her top up over her head. He stared for a moment at her naked torso before his hand, almost reverently, touched her breast again. "You are so beautiful," he whispered.

Their hands explored each other, lingering over areas that produced the most reaction. Luca's lips were busy, too, exploring and tasting curves as if he were sampling delicacies from a buffet. He slipped her shorts from her, his hands fluttering over the scars on her buttocks.

Awash with sensation, she managed to lever her eyes open when he whispered her name. He hovered above her, searching her face.

"*Amore*, this may hurt, I am so sorry." His voice was thick. His body glistened with a sheen of moisture, his eyes blazed with passion, yet still he thought of her comfort.

Luca stopped moving at her sharp intake of breath. She searched his face. He seemed to be concentrating hard to keep still, allowing her body time to get used to him. The pain receded, and she hesitantly moved beneath him. He withdrew slowly. Worried that he would stop, Sophia grabbed his buttocks as if they were a lifeline in a swollen river.

"*Amore, tesoro mio*, do not worry. I am not going anywhere," he whispered against her lips. He kissed her deeply as he slowly entered her again. This time there was no pain. Instead waves of pleasure radiated from her core to the tips of her toes. Her legs were wrapped around Luca's back. She squeezed him tighter, but still he kept up the slow rhythm, until she had to bite her tongue to stop a scream. She called out his name with what seemed to be the last breath in her body.

Luca increased the pace until she gave up all

pretense of being in control and allowed the sensations to carry her to a distant shore. Suddenly the world exploded into light and her whole body vibrated. A minute later Luca went taut. He whispered unintelligible words into her ear, over and over as if unable to stop himself.

She drifted back to reality slowly, still in awe at what had transpired between them. Olivia had told her that when it was good, it was earthmoving. But nothing had prepared her for the spectacular, time-stopping pleasure she'd experienced with Luca. Not a single thought of England had been able to form in her overwhelmed brain.

• • •

When Luca eventually opened his eyes the next morning, the room was aglow with soft sunshine. He'd slept deeply, finally satiated for the first time since meeting Sophia. Reaching for her, he was surprised to find the bed empty, and a flash of panic raced through him. He couldn't have dreamed such pleasure, such a connection with his beautiful wife.

Sitting upright, his relief was palpable to find that the events of the night hadn't been another dream. The sheets were askew and the blankets tumbled off the bed. His clothes were neatly folded on the chair across the room. A faint splash of water revealed the location of his delectable wife.

He lay back in bed, reliving the highlights of the night before. Never in his life had he experienced such passion, such pleasure. More than just a physical release, it was as if a dam had burst in his very core, swamping his body with emotion.

He threw back the sheet at another splashing sound and went in search of his wife. She was stretched out in the bath, her eyes closed, a Mona Lisa smile on her lips. A thin layer of bubbles obscured her body from view, but like seductive lingerie, it lured him to join her.

A shower man, he'd questioned the expense to restore the wrought iron tub when he'd renovated. He hadn't taken a bath since he'd been a child. With Sophia in the water, every last euro was money well spent.

"Mind if I join you?" He didn't wait for her reply and stepped into the warm water.

Sophia opened her eyes, and her lips parted in a surprised expression. Her gaze ran the length of him, lingering for a long, hot moment on his groin where his blood began to pool once more. An answering flame of desire heated her eyes. This may be a quick bath.

"I take that as a yes," he replied. She moved her legs over so he could sit, but he wanted more body contact. He'd waited long enough; he was no longer content to just look at Sophia. He needed to touch her, have her touch him. "Here, let me scrub your back." She shifted in the bath so her back was facing him. He picked up her sponge but soon discarded it in favor of using his hands.

When the water sloshed out of the bathtub for the third time, he lifted her out and gently placed her on her feet before him. She reached for her towel to dry herself off, but he had a better idea. The heat from their bodies soon evaporated any water left on her skin after his hands and lips had passed over her. When she melted against him, he swung her into his arms and carried her back to the bed.

This morning their lovemaking had a frantic pace to it; they couldn't get enough of each other. When finally they climaxed together, an involuntary scream came from Sophia and a loud groan of completion from him. She hid her face in his chest, but he wasn't going to let her become ashamed of her pleasure. A timid smile played on her lips when her eyes finally met his.

"Your mother is going to be pounding on the door soon, asking what's going on," she said shyly.

"The only question my mother will be asking is when she can expect her first grandchild."

Sophia stiffened in his arms. "We'd better get up. I'm starving."

"Me too," he said, nibbling on her ear. He began to trail love bites down her neck when she pushed him back.

"I mean it, Luca. You can't keep me prisoner here in bed without feeding me. It's against the Geneva Convention." Her breathy voice contradicted the seriousness of her words.

"The Geneva Convention only applies to prisoners of war, not prisoners of lovemaking. But alright, let's get something to eat."

She rolled off him. Cool air replaced her body warmth and he repressed a shiver. He flung back the sheets and followed his wife.

"Good God, Luca, it's almost nine o'clock. You're late for work." She'd wrapped a satin dressing gown around her but he could see where her nipples pressed against the silky fabric. He forced his eyes to her face, which still held a pink glow from their recent activities. Her hair framed her face, in wild abandon. He didn't care if he never went into work again.

"I'll work from home today. With my mother here, they'll understand in the office." Still he stared.

"Oh, it's because your mother is here that you're staying, is it?" She undid the belt and let the robe drop to the floor with a seductive laugh.

"That is the official story. You know the real reason is because I cannot bear to leave you."

"I guess we won't be going on honeymoon on the weekend though. Now that your mother is visiting and … well … we've already done it."

He flipped on the shower and grabbed her as she walked past, pulling her into the warm spray. "Oh, we're still going. Mamma will be fine. Thierry, her husband, is coming tomorrow, and she won't even notice we're gone. Plus, I want two days with you and only you."

She put her arms around his neck and kissed him. It was another half hour before they were both dressed and made their way downstairs.

• • •

"*Buongiorno*, Sophia. Did you sleep well?" Giada had a huge smile on her face as she asked the question. After a quick breakfast in the kitchen, Sophia had found her mother-in-law enjoying the morning sun on the terrace. Maria had brought out a fancy coffee set and put it on the table.

Sophia didn't look up from pouring her coffee until she was sure she had her smile under control. "Very well, Mamma Giada. And you?"

"Yes, thank you."

Luca strolled out onto the terrace and wrapped his arms around her from the back. He pressed a kiss where her neck met her shoulder, sending a zap of electricity through her.

"Luca, you have not gone to work?" Giada's smile increased.

"You should be a lawyer, Mama. You ask questions you already know the answers to," Luca replied. He released Sophia and filled his coffee cup before sitting on the arm of her chair.

"I am just surprised. I have not known you to take a day off work in years. You even worked on my wedding day."

"I am working today as well. Just from home. I want to make sure you don't scare away my wife with all your questions." Luca ran his hand down her hair, and Sophia had to force herself not to trail her hand along his firm thigh. He'd given her another orgasm in the shower, although he hadn't entered her, saying she was going to be sore enough as it was, having just lost her virginity. But it was such a delicious ache.

Her eyes closed as she remembered the pleasure. They snapped open when his mother spoke again. "My only question is when I'm going to be a *nonna*?"

Luca's eyes met hers with suppressed laughter. She had never seen him so lighthearted. He looked years younger and so gorgeous, she inhaled sharply. "I think we should make Mamma wait one year for every time she asks us about grandbabies. What do you say, Sophia?"

"I say you should go to work and leave your mother and me to talk."

He leaned down and kissed her lightly on the lips. "As you wish. But if she gets too nosey, tell her to mind her own affairs."

She flicked her eyes to Giada, knowing she'd never have the guts to tell off her mother-in-law. The pure delight in the other woman's eyes set Sophia at ease. Seeing her son so happy had done a lot to give their relationship a good start.

Luca left the terrace, whistling.

"He is so happy. I worried he would be too busy at work to find a wife."

"He does work a lot, but we're dealing with it." Well, trying to.

Giada picked up a magazine from the glass-topped table. "I had a stop-over in London and bought some magazines. Maybe you would like to read something from home?"

Sophia picked up the other magazine from the table. Her stomach roiled as she stared at the cover. An icy chill gripped her, despite the warm sunshine. The euphoria that had her floating burst like a bubble, hurtling her back to reality.

She glanced again at the magazine. Maybe it had been a mistake, an image conjured up by the mention of her past last night. No such luck. Staring at her from the cover of the magazine was Kathy Summers, the girl who had been the final catalyst in destroying her childhood. She repressed a shudder—she was older now and stronger. Sophia flipped the magazine over and stood.

"Maybe later. I'm going to take a stroll through the garden. I love the scent of the flowers in the morning air. Would you like to come with me?"

Chapter Ten

"Luca, can you help me with this?" Sophia emerged from the bathroom, struggling to pull up the zipper on the back of her soft blue silk dress. It was sleeveless with a sweetheart neckline. Fitted down to the thigh, it then fell in soft folds to her knees.

They'd arrived at Villa d'Este earlier that afternoon. As he'd said, Giada hadn't seemed to mind that they were going away so soon after her arrival. Her husband had arrived the previous evening, and Giada had been like a giggly school girl, excited to see him, even though they'd only been apart a couple days.

"You know, only the promise that soon I will be unzipping this dress allows my fingers to do this. Helping you put on your clothes goes against every fiber of my being." Luca's breath was hot against her ear and when he kissed her neck, making her knees wobble. It took every ounce of willpower she had to step away from him.

She grabbed the matching wrap and took a moment to admire him. He was dressed in a gray suit with a white shirt and pale pink tie. His black hair was brushed back and her fingers itched to run through it and release the curls. She preferred him slightly disheveled, a satisfied smile on his face. In private anyway. Now he looked every inch the powerful businessman, intent on securing the deal. Only tonight's business was pleasure. Another shiver coursed through her already sensitized body. They may have had two nights together already, but that didn't mean she'd had enough of him, or, it seemed, him of her.

The maître'd sat them at a table on the terrace, next to the lake. She took a quick look at the menu handed to her, but her thoughts were too jumbled to decipher the contents. "I can't decide what to eat; it all looks so good. Would you order for me, Luca? I'd like a surprise, something I haven't had before." Tonight seemed like the perfect time to try new things.

Luca ordered their meal while she stared at the twinkling lights across the lake. "If you like surprises, then you should appreciate this." He handed her a small velvet box.

They had exchanged wedding bands at the registrar's office, but he'd not given her an engagement ring. She hadn't really thought anything of it. Jewelry wasn't a big thing for her, probably because she'd never had anything of value. With slightly shaking hands, she opened the small box and her hand flew to her throat.

"Oh, Luca, it's exquisite," she breathed. Inside the box lay a large pear-shaped, faceted emerald surrounded by smaller diamonds on a gold band. The cut of the stones looked old; however, the brilliance of the gems gave it a timeless elegance.

"I know it's not a huge diamond like you were probably expecting and deserve. I will buy you those as well. This is the family ring. My father gave it to my mother, and his father before him. It has passed down to the first male to give his bride for over a hundred years. My mother has been keeping it for me. She gave it to me this afternoon to give to you."

"It is the most beautiful ring I've ever seen. I will treasure it until the day I hand it over to our son to give to his bride." The legacy of the piece was almost overwhelming. She'd never had anything with family tradition to add to its value

Luca slid the ring on her finger and then raised her hand and placed a slow kiss on it, all the while holding her gaze—his eyes promising much more of the unexpected.

Without her even noticing, the waiter placed their first course on the table. She lifted a taste of the creamy soup to her mouth when a chill coursed down her spine.

"Sophia? Sophia Stevens? Is that really you?" A husky voice with a polished English accent called out.

She dropped the spoon as if scalded. It clattered against the china bowl, spewing its contents across the place setting.

Seven years. How could she still remember the voice after seven years? How could it cause terror to well up in her heart after all this time? She'd thought she'd exorcised that particular ghost, and now it had come back to haunt her in the flesh. Seeing her face on the magazine a couple of days ago had been bad, hearing her voice now was worse.

Luca glanced at her as she grabbed his hand and squeezed tightly. Black spots danced before her, obscuring his concerned face. She tried to reassure him with a smile, but it never formed. Before she could even take in a shaky breath, the owner of the voice appeared at their table.

The woman was tall with long, blonde hair, the color as natural as a Saharan waterfall. She wore heavy makeup and a deep red dress that left little to the imagination. The neckline, if it could be called that, as it was nowhere near her neck, revealed an abundant amount of breast, which Sophia would bet were not natural either. The hemline only made it to mid-thigh, showing an ample amount of leg, teetering on strappy sandals with six-inch heels. A cloud of Poison perfume enveloped her, an apt choice of scent given the wearer's venomous personality.

"Kathy Summers." Sophia exhaled sharply. It was as though someone had punched her in the stomach, she was barely able to breathe. Trying to stop herself from shaking, she squeezed Luca's hand tighter.

"Actually, I'm called Kate now—now that I'm famous," the other woman said smugly. She tossed her hair over her shoulder and turned a blinding white smile on Luca.

"Yes, I've seen your face, and other *assets*, in the papers. But I don't remember you having such a posh accent. Whatever happened to your north London drawl?" She waited while the actress stopped devouring Luca with her eyes and looked at her once again.

"Ah, we're a long way from Tottenham now, dahling." Kathy wrinkled her nose, as if disgusted to be reminded of her past. "What are you doing in Italy, Sophia? I almost didn't recognize you."

"I'm not surprised." The bile that rose from her

stomach tinged her words with bitterness. The blood that had drained from her face earlier came back in full force as a flash of pure anger and hatred filled her. "The last time I saw you, you were covered in my blood."

• • •

Luca's stomach clenched at Sophia's words. Was his wife in danger? He started to rise from his seat but sat back down as her grip on him tightened. Her eyes begged him not to escalate the already unpleasant scene.

He recognized the woman from the restaurant in London. The one who had caused Sophia to flee on that occasion as well. He'd looked her up; she was some sort of B-list British soap star, known more for her body than her acting ability. But he still had no idea where she fit into Sophia's past.

"Yes, well, that's ancient history." The artificially enhanced actress looked around as if to make sure no one else heard Sophia's comment.

"Not when you look at the scars every day." Sophia's jaw clenched at the words. "I think your *friends* are looking for you." She indicated the group of people waving at Kate.

"Well, I guess I'll see you around." Kate dismissed Sophia with a nod but flashed another dazzling smile at him. She sauntered over to her dinner companions with an exaggerated swing of her hips.

Sophia was extremely pale. Although she was making a valiant effort to hold herself together, she started to twitch. His heart burned.

"I, um, I need to leave. I have to get out of here, get away from her. Please," she looked beseechingly at him, "please, can we go home?"

"Yes, of course." He rose and helped her out of her chair. Her whole body was shaking now and he kept his arm around her for support. "Come to the car. Someone will collect our things tomorrow."

Within minutes, Sophia sat in the passenger seat of the Maserati, cocooned in a blanket he'd pulled out of the back. He stole quick glances at her as he wove through the streets of the town, noting that she was still pale. At least the trembling had stopped. Once they were on the motorway, he stepped on the accelerator and the powerful car hungrily ate up the miles. Soon they were pulling through the gates of the villa and into the driveway.

His stepfather appeared at the top of the stairs, wearing only a burgundy dressing gown, as they entered the hallway. He held a phone in his hands.

"It is okay, Thierry," Luca reassured the other man. "It is just us, no need to call the police."

Thierry took one look at Sophia's distressed expression and didn't inquire the reason for their unexpected return. "Sure, call up if you need us," he replied before returning to the bedroom.

"Come into the snug; it is more comfortable," Luca said. He gently steered Sophia toward the room at the back of the house. "I will get you a brandy to help calm your nerves."

He poured the drinks while he struggled to come up with some way to comfort his wife. Should he encourage her to talk or simply hold her so she knew he was there for her? He wasn't equipped to deal with such deep emotional trauma. This wasn't something that could be fixed with a hammer and nails or a bridging loan. Being a businessman now wasn't going to help. He needed to be a husband.

Glancing at her reflection in the mirror over the fireplace, he could almost see Sophia shrinking back within herself. Was her independence a protection, a way to shield herself from further hurt? Maybe it wasn't that she didn't want him in her life. Perhaps she was afraid to let him in because she'd been hurt by someone close to her before. Any progress they'd made in their relationship, the understanding, the partnership would all disappear if he failed her now. He took a deep breath and got ready to fight for their future.

• • •

Sophia sank into the overstuffed sofa, breathing a little easier now that she was home. Taking the brandy snifter Luca offered her, she motioned for him to sit next to her. She wanted his arms around her, to feel the safety of his embrace. As if sensing her need, he pulled her against him, rubbing her arm up and down.

The amber liquid burned as it went down her throat before settling in her stomach. Comforting warmth infused her whole body. After a couple of sips, she felt able to unclench her fist without her body starting to shake again.

"I'm so sorry I spoiled our honeymoon," she said at

last, her voice hesitant and unsteady.

"I am not worried about that," Luca replied. "I am worried about you. Can you tell me what happened?"

Her heart beat faster. He'd left the beautiful hotel without any questions, not even asking why. Not considering her a fool for getting upset so easily.

"I think I'd better start at the beginning … with my family," she began. She'd tried so hard to distance herself from her past, yet it always caught up with her. Even 900 kilometers away it found her, threatening to destroy her current life. She took a deep breath.

"My parents, Charlie and Janice, married young. My dad worked as a bricklayer and my mum had come down from Manchester to pursue her dreams of being an actress in the theatre. They met at a football match. They were cheering for opposite teams but were seated next to each other. By the end of the game, they were madly in love and Dad for once didn't care that his team lost.

"Neither of their families were particularly pleased with the marriage, and I don't remember ever seeing my grandparents. My parents didn't have much, only their dreams. Mum was still auditioning for parts in various productions and Dad had ideas of running his own construction company." If she told her story as though it had happened to someone else, she could keep it together. Some days, especially since she started living in Italy, it almost felt like it was someone else's life. She paused, trying to put her jumbled thoughts in order.

"After a few years, my brother Ben came along, followed within a year by my second brother, Paul. Shortly after Paul was born, my dad had an accident at work. He fell off some scaffolding and broke his hips and both legs. For a while they weren't sure he'd be able to walk again. He managed that, but couldn't work anymore as a brickie. I guess it was then that Mum realized she would never be an actress and now she had to support her family. With no real training or experience, so took whatever jobs she could get.

"I was born when Paul was three years old. By this time the family was living mostly on social benefit. My dad practically lived at the pub or at football matches. He always found money to attend the games. Sometimes he would do some work to make a little extra to go to the away matches, all the while collecting the dole. My mum worked part time at the local grocery store and did a few cleaning jobs.

"When I was three, my sister Sarah was born and two years later James came along. We were five children living in a three-bed council flat in north London. The lift always smelled of pee, and the stairwell was the location of daily drug deals." She rubbed her eyes, trying to rid herself of the images in her head. Taking another sip of the brandy, she hoped its warmth would burn away the emptiness inside.

"By the time James was born, my dad had almost completely opted out of family life. When he was home he was watching the telly, or more usually fast asleep in front of it. As soon as Mum came home from work, he was off to the pub. I used to lie awake at night, waiting to hear the door open and close, to know he was home safe before I could fall asleep. Dad never shouted; he never hit us. He just ignored our existence—quite a feat in a small flat with five children.

"Mum tried to be a good parent, but she was always tired. And looking back now, I realize, drained by disappointment. She'd make us tea—fish fingers and chips or something out of a can. Mum didn't really cook, which is why I never learned. As soon as Ben was old enough to look after us, she, too, went out most evenings, over to her sister's house a few streets away, coming home in time to tuck us into bed, most nights."

"Why didn't your aunt come over to your place if she lived so close?" Luca looked into her eyes, as if to reassure her, to show his concern.

"My aunt didn't like children. She never married and preferred the quiet life; she was a bookkeeper for a local business. Auntie had a nice little terraced house and hated coming to the 'nasty flat' as she called it." Sophia took a deep breath and continued with her story.

"Ben, my oldest brother, was wonderful. He was only a child himself, yet he helped us younger ones with our homework. He taught James to read. He would put on puppet shows behind the sofa using Dad's socks and an oven mitt. He always had a smile and knew how to cheer us up. Most of the boys his age were down the park playing football; Ben was at home reading us stories using funny voices for the characters." She smiled at the memories, but there were tears in her eyes. Luca ran his hand down her hair, offering her comfort.

"If something exciting happened at school, or if we did well on a test, it was Ben we told, not our parents. All our hopes and dreams or daily disappointments we laid at Ben's door. He was so young for such responsibility, yet he never complained. He never told us to get lost or find someone else to talk to. He would've been such an amazing dad." Her voice caught on the last sentence. Telling Luca was harder than she'd expected. She couldn't pretend her past didn't matter when his strong arms were around her, providing the security she'd so desperately needed then. The comfort she so desperately needed now. If he pulled away, she'd fall apart. And she wasn't sure she could put the pieces back together again.

Instead, Luca lifted her so she was sitting across his lap. She put her empty brandy snifter down on the coffee table and leaned back. The steady beat of his heart against her ear, and the warmth of his body against hers, gave her the strength to continue.

"Paul was a bit rebellious. He didn't like sitting at home with a 'bunch of babies,' as he used to call us. He would go and hang out with his friends, quite often getting in trouble. But he always managed to slip in the door minutes before Mum came home, pretending he'd been there the whole time. Paul was very clever, and though he never seemed to do any homework or studying he always had good grades, so Mum and Dad thought nothing was wrong.

"I was the cleaner. I used to clean the house spotless so Mum wouldn't have to do it when she came home. I hoped it would make her happy and make her want to stay with us. I was always annoyed at the other children for making a mess. Paul used to call me uptight. I guess it was my way with coping. At least my surroundings could be clean, neat, tidy, orderly, even if my life was a mess.

"Sarah cried a lot, always whining and complaining. I think she was starved for affection. That's probably why, even today, if a man shows any interest in her, she immediately falls in love with him. She's always lurching from one bad relationship into another." Despite being only three years apart, she'd never felt very close to her sister. They were polar opposites in temperament. She'd always thought Sarah's sensitivity a weakness. Now, however, having had a taste of Luca's tenderness, she could understand her sister a little more.

"James, my younger brother, was beautiful. He had curly, blonde hair and bright blue eyes and dimples when he smiled, which was often. People used to stop in the street when we walked by and comment on what a beautiful child he was." Her voice broke and she took a deep, shuddering breath.

"I don't think I'll ever complain again about being an only child," Luca commented.

"Oh, it wasn't all bad. I do have some happy childhood memories. Paul once stole ten pounds out of his friend's mother's purse. But then he felt guilty for doing it. So rather than buy smokes, which had been his intention, we went to the park and he bought us all chips and ice cream." She smiled genuinely for the first time since meeting Kathy. Getting all this off her chest made her heart was a little lighter. Luca held her tightly, one hand rubbing her back in a comforting gesture. Maybe he wouldn't be put off by her past, consider her unworthy.

"Things went okay for a couple of years. We all did

pretty well in school. Paul got selected for the track team and so had something more positive to focus his energies on. Although Mum and Dad were still kind of living their own lives, the rest of us were close-knit and we got on as best we could. We were five children living in a small space, so of course there were fights. Yet somehow, instinctively I guess, we all knew we had to stick together to survive." She took a deep breath and barely whispered the words. "But when things went bad, they went bad very quick."

Chapter Eleven

Sophia's shudder went straight through Luca. Her pain became his. It was the first time he was truly connected to his wife, outside of the bedroom. The depth of his desire to protect her surprised him. He hadn't realized how much he wanted her to need him, to rely on him, to trust him. He pulled her closer, and she rested her head on his chest for a moment.

"You do not have to tell me more, *tesoro mio*."

"No, I want you to know it all. I just need a minute."

She pulled out of his arms and paced the room, obviously too emotional to sit still. She paused by the fireplace mantel and rearranged the photos symmetrically. Finally, she turned toward him, but her eyes didn't meet his. She tucked a strand of hair behind her ear. He knew their relationship would never progress unless she unburdened herself—trusted him with her secret. But it was hard to watch her build her walls again.

Sophia took a deep breath as though bracing herself for rejection. "When Ben was seventeen, he fell in love with a girl at school. She was pretty but vain. Ben had spent the last five years looking after his younger siblings rather than playing football or hanging out with his peers, so he was a bit scrawny and quiet. This girl didn't appreciate his sensitive nature or the incredible responsibility he'd shouldered without complaint. She rejected him outright, even mocking his attempts to win her heart. Worse, she made him the laughingstock of the school. Poor Ben, he was so dejected." Sophia's voice was soft and distant, lost in the past.

"Was it the woman from Lake Como?" He was trying to work out where she fit into the story and why she had caused so much panic in Sophia, not once but twice.

"No, I can't even remember this girl's name, and I don't think I ever met her. But Ben couldn't get over her. He followed her around the school and watched her from a distance everywhere she went. I guess finally he got the message that it was never going to happen. One day I came home from school to find Ben lying on the floor of the flat, unconscious. I couldn't rouse him and was about to call for an ambulance when Paul came home. He'd seen it before and knew what to do. Ben had passed out from a drug overdose. When he came around, he begged us not to tell anyone. He said it had been a one-off thing and he'd learned his lesson and would never do drugs again … but he did."

Luca wanted to go to her, to take her in his arms, yet he sensed that she needed to stand alone to tell him. To exorcise whatever demons still haunted her by wandering about the room. She moved over to the window. Her face was reflected in the glass, her eyes lifeless, caught up in the memories. She cleared her throat and continued.

"Ben started stealing, first from home, selling anything worth anything to get money for drugs—then from our neighbors and friends, the local shops. Paul and

I tried to talk to him, but I was thirteen and Paul was sixteen. Ben had been acting like our parent for so long, he didn't think he needed to listen to us. I think Mum knew something was wrong, although she never said anything. About six months after I found Ben on the floor from the overdose, the doorbell rang at six in the morning.

"I knew it was the police—I thought they'd come to arrest Ben for stealing, and in a way I was relieved. I thought then maybe he would be able to get the help he desperately needed.

"I answered the door and sure enough there were two police officers there. But instead of asking for Ben, they asked for Mum and Dad. I woke them up and then listened at the sitting room door as they told my parents that Ben had been found dead in a known drug house. Mum started crying … Dad couldn't believe it, he had no idea that Ben had been into drugs. They left shortly after to identify the body. My aunt came and stayed with us while they were gone. I don't think any one of us said a single word until they returned and confirmed the news. It was like being in a nightmare, where you can't speak, can't scream … but there was no waking up from this bad dream."

Sophia's voice was quieter now and she returned to the fireplace, as though seeking out its warmth even though it wasn't on. She wrapped her arms around herself and paused for a moment. He had to stop himself from getting off the sofa and pulling her down beside him—she seemed so distant, so lost. He ached for her.

"I don't remember the funeral, except feeling numb.

Ben was the one I told when I was happy, sad, scared. People kept telling me I should cry, but I couldn't. There was nobody there anymore to hold me and tell me it was going to get better."

Sophia shrugged, but her eyes were bleak.

"For a few months after Ben's death, Mum and Dad actually spent some time with us children. I think Dad even went on a school trip with James. Although I missed Ben dreadfully, it looked like things had at least changed for the better in our family. However, within six months it was back to normal. Dad was out at the pub, or with his mates, and Mum was either at work or over at Auntie's house. Paul tried to take Ben's place, but he didn't have the same temperament. Ben had always been gentle and kind, Paul was more of a hothead. He had no patience, especially for Sarah, who cried even more now that Ben was gone.

"Before long Paul was away from home as much as Dad and Mum. He was missing from school, too. Soon it was apparent he'd joined a gang. I tried to talk to him … he said he was attempting to find out who had sold Ben the bad drugs and once he did, he would leave the gang. I was scared, first Ben now Paul. I was still the cleaner, trying my best to look after Sarah and James.

"About a year after Ben died, Paul came home late one night, covered in blood. I watched him through the crack in my bedroom door as he tried to clean himself up in the bathroom, across the hall. I guess he didn't want to turn on any more lights in case he woke someone up, so he kept the door open and used the hall light that was always on, as Sarah was afraid of the dark. He made such a mess. Isn't it strange how even a little blood can make such a big mess? I remember wondering how I was going to clean it up before Mum and Dad woke up."

Sophia was so remote now, he almost didn't recognize her. It was as though she was telling someone else's story. Luca didn't know whether he should encourage her to go on, to get it all out, or stop her now and continue another time. She let out a long sigh and continued.

"Before I could even get up in the morning, the police were banging on the door. I didn't answer it this time. I hid in my room. But the walls were paper thin, and I could hear everything. Paul was arrested for murdering one of the gang members and also another boy, who the police think witnessed the first killing, and was stabbed to keep him quiet. They had Paul's image on CCTV camera, and with the blood all over his clothes and most of the bathroom it was a pretty open and shut case.

"Our family was notorious and people even crossed the street to avoid us. School was a nightmare. Fortunately, Sarah and especially James were still a little too young to fully understand what was going on. There was talk that they would be taken into care, so Dad promised to be at home when they finished school and stay until at least Mum returned. A promise he actually kept. I think for the first time he realized what was happening to the family."

"What about you? How did you cope?" Luca found it almost impossible to get the words out. The distress Sophia had experienced certainly put the bullying he'd endured into perspective.

"I no longer had any friends, so there was nothing to do but study and read. With the evidence against Paul, it took only six months to bring the case to trial. It was terrible, even harder than when Ben had died. I was a witness, having seen Paul come home covered in blood. I didn't want to grass on my brother; however, I also believe in Justice. If Paul took an innocent life, then he should undergo some form of punishment. I didn't really care about the gang member; I figured he had made his own choices. I kept thinking about the poor boy who was in the wrong place at the wrong time. He'd been fifteen when he was killed, same age I was. But it didn't stop the guilt; I felt like I was betraying my brother.

"I was in school the day the sentence was announced. Of course by lunchtime the whole school knew Paul was going to prison for twelve years. I went to the loo to try to compose myself, when a group of my former friends came in, including Kathy Summers, the woman we saw at Villa d'Este."

Sophia started to shake. He stood and pulled her into his arms, holding her head close to his chest.

"They grabbed me and pushed me to the ground and a couple of girls sat on me so I couldn't move. Someone stuffed a school tie in my mouth so I couldn't scream. Then Kathy carved the initials of the boy who had been killed into my buttocks with a pen knife. They were discussing doing worse to me when one of them I guess felt squeamish from all the blood and ran to get a teacher. Funny, I don't remember the pain, but I can still smell the floor cleaner. To this day I can't stand pine-scented cleaning products. Anyway, someone called an ambulance and that was the last time I set foot in that school."

"*Amore*, it is enough. The memories are making you too upset." He was shaking now as well and moved them both to the sofa to sit down. His arm tightened around her as if he could protect her from the pain of her former life.

"No, I have to finish. I want you to know it all, to know all my horrible past. Then if you want to end the marriage, I will go quietly back to England. It's probably too late to get an annulment. I should have told you before we married that my brother was a murderer."

"I want to know only so I can understand you better. Your family, your history, makes no difference to me." At least now he understood her desire to leave England and never look back.

Sophia's tears ran down her cheeks and fell onto her clenched fist. She stared at the wetness on her hand, as if unsure of where it came from. "It took eighty stitches to close up the wounds and I couldn't sit for a long time. You've seen the scars. In the hospital I met Olivia. I won't tell you her story; that's her business. Needless to say, she'd been through worse. She was a little younger than me, she'd only just turned fifteen.

"We decided to run away. We lived on the streets for a few months, sleeping in turns so one of us could keep an eye out for danger. There was no time to look back, no time for dreams and what ifs. Our only thoughts were for survival. We stole food—fruit from the market and stuff like that."

"What about your parents? Surely they must have looked for you?" He was shocked. Never had he thought his quiet, serene wife fought for survival on the street.

"My parents made an effort to find me. But I sent them a letter saying I needed a new start. Dad was looking after Sarah and James now, so they didn't need me. I couldn't go back. I didn't want to be the parent and end up like Ben or Paul. I was selfish. I just wanted to be responsible for me. Those girls in school had killed the old Sophia, as much as my brother had killed that boy."

"What about Olivia's family? Couldn't you have gone to them?"

"Olivia's mother never even reported her missing. I was all Olivia had, and sometimes that is what kept me going—knowing that without me she would be all alone. Olivia and I were inseparable, since the day we met in the hospital we've been each other's family."

"*Dio mio.*"

"Finally, after one too-close call, we sought refuge at a youth shelter. They took us in without questions, offered us counseling. They helped us finish our education and get jobs. I don't even want to think what would have become of us if we hadn't gone there. After I got work and a place to live, I tried to help out by volunteering when I had any free time."

"What about Sarah and James?" He was still finding it hard to believe his wife's resilience, although he should have known from the way she'd adapted so quickly to life in a foreign country. She said she'd been afraid to lose control, and now he knew why. Because there had been no one to protect her in the past. His arms tightened around her.

"I checked in on them, mostly from a distance for the first couple of years. I didn't want to go home and give my dad an excuse to exit out of their lives again. Sarah has a lot of issues. She'd sleep with any boy who showed interest in her and was pregnant by the time she was sixteen. Her second baby was born when she was eighteen. Men are in and out of her life, most of them losers. She just had her third baby and that father has already left.

"James finished school last year. He's doing okay. I want him to have a trade, something that would ensure he could always get work. So I'm helping him pay for college. He's going to be an electrician and still lives at home. Mum is pretty sick at the moment, so he does most of the cooking and cleaning.

"I have great hopes for James. Although I still picture him as the curly haired, blue eyed cherub and have trouble seeing him as the six-foot man he is today. I keep in touch with him. I'm hoping maybe he can come out here for a couple of weeks, if Mum's well enough. Once I break the news to him of our marriage, that is."

"When do you think that will be?" He'd been curious why she hadn't told her family about their marriage. Now he understood all too well. And it wasn't good news for their relationship. She'd been independent and strong for so long that getting her to let him in would take time.

"Probably sooner rather than later. James is finishing up his courses right now and about to start his apprenticeship. But I know he wants to have a little break before he starts work full-time. I thought I'd tell him when he got his results, and then invite him to come over, if that's okay with you."

"Absolutely. I would love to meet him, and any others in your family you want to invite. Maybe Sarah and her children could use a holiday." He said this genuinely. Although Sophia didn't currently want to spend much time with her family, other than James, that might change as their own children arrived.

"Maybe. I'm not sure if your quiet little household here is ready for Sarah and her brood." Sophia let out a deep breath, her shoulders higher as if the secret of her family had weighed heavily on her.

"*Amore*, you are amazing. Thank you for trusting me with your story."

Now he knew why she'd married him. But it wasn't enough. He needed her to need him. To want to be with him for more than his money. He had to figure out how he could get her to rebuild her life around him and not grant him access only on occasion. He wanted her to stop pretending and be real.

Because one thing had become clear over the past month. Their marriage was becoming more than a business arrangement to him. The little voice in his head chimed in with a chorus of "I told you so." Yet it offered no advice on how he could make an independent woman need him.

Maybe it was time for another plan.

Chapter Twelve

"Sophia, is there something you want to tell me?"

She closed the book she'd been reading and put it down on the table next to the chaise, trying to buy some time before answering. She'd been so careful over the last couple of weeks not to show how much she was coming to care for her husband, or how much she wanted him to need her in return. Could he have guessed? Sometimes she surprised herself with her acting ability. She must have inherited it from her mother.

She searched Luca's face, trying to discern the reason for his question. His eyes were impassive, not showing the warmth or desire she was used to seeing in them recently. He held a paper in his hand.

"Can you give me a hint?"

His face was remote, as if he was trying to distance himself from some unwanted emotion. "This is the statement for your credit card," he offered, between clenched teeth.

She tried to remember any outrageous purchases but failed. The bills for the clothes she'd bought with Isabella had come through a month ago without the merest hint of a question from Luca. Aside from the reupholstered sofa for the sitting room, which Luca claimed to love, she hadn't bought anything major for the house either. She hoped one day she and Luca could shop together for a new dining set. Something they chose together, a symbol of their unity. Not what they currently were—two disparate people who had amazing sex.

"Have I spent too much?"

Luca's face was still blank, although a muscle throbbed in his jaw.

"There is a charge on here for a business license."

"Oh right, I forgot about that, I didn't have any cash the day I applied, so had to put the charge on the card. Don't worry, once I get the finances sorted, I'll put the expense through my new company." The business license had only cost 100 euro. She still didn't understand why Luca was upset.

"Do you not think you could have talked to me about starting a business?" His accent became more pronounced.

"You've been so preoccupied lately, I didn't want to bother you with something so trivial. And I told you I was bored sitting at home. I finished my interior design course and got my certificate. And Jonathan was really happy with the work I did for him and gave me an amazing reference. So I put an advertisement in the local British ex-pat newspaper and quite a few people have contacted me. I thought getting a business license was the proper thing to do. It seems a lot of work is done here under the table, but I didn't want to get involved in anything shady. I know how important your reputation is to you." The frostiness in her tone surprised even her. He'd made it abundantly clear that his reputation was more important than her happiness.

"I assumed you would abide by our arrangement."

The chill in his voice matched hers.

She leapt to her feet, anger incinerating her normal passivity to white-hot fury in an instant. How dare Luca accuse her of breaking their agreement? Despite all their recent intimacy, did he still regard their marriage as a business deal?

"When I agreed to this *marriage,* I clearly recall you saying that I could continue my education, even get a degree." The sound of her heart breaking temporarily drowned out the thudding of her pulse in her ears.

"An education, yes. Starting a business is different. If my wife is having to take work, the gossip will be that my company is failing. A rumor like that can do serious damage to my reputation."

"Maybe you should worry more about me, and less about rumors," she shot back.

"I do care about you. I don't want to see you stressed. You won't have time to work when the babies start to come."

The crushing sensation in Sophia's chest intensified. Clearly Luca only made love to her to get her pregnant. The lust she thought she saw in him wasn't craving for her, but simply a desire to have a child.

"Your mother told me she was married to your father for four years before your birth, and that despite her wishes, you were an only child. Do you expect me to sit around for years twiddling my thumbs, waiting for a baby that may never even happen?"

The fury that entered Luca's eyes at her words made her step back.

"My father was nearly fifty years old when he

married my mother. I assure you, I will have no such difficulty in fathering a child." With that pronouncement he turned on his heel and left the terrace, balling up the credit card bill and flinging it into the corner on his way out.

She fell back onto the chaise. The late-spring sunshine no longer warmed her. Anger ebbed away, leaving only pain. Once again her dreams had come crashing down. This time, though, there had been no warning. The past two weeks had been almost idyllic. Revealing her past to Luca had been liberating. She now saw herself as capable of being the wife he wanted. And it had given her the confidence to seize her dream and start her own business, knowing that even if she failed, she'd have Luca's respect for trying. Or so she'd thought.

Since Giada and Thierry had returned to Corsica, Sophia's days had slipped into a quiet routine. In the morning she would work in the garden with Vittore or do some baking in the kitchen with Maria. After *riposo* she often visited reclamation yards, antique markets or second hand stores with Jonathan or Isabella. She needed something to keep her thoughts off her husband, before they became all-consuming and she lost herself. Even then, she had spent each hour waiting for Luca to come home from work.

Her evening and nights had also entered a routine, although not one she would describe as quiet. Much to Maria's delight, and hers, Luca was often home for dinner. They would spend an enjoyable evening, often with her curled up in a chair in the study reading, while he caught up on some paperwork or answered email messages.

The nights, however, were a different matter. Passion flared easily and often, and she usually fell into an exhausted sleep, still wrapped in Luca's arms. She'd been able to convince herself that her marriage was more than just a business arrangement—that Luca cared for her, or at least was starting to. Now, however, she knew it was all a complete sham.

The roar of the Maserati's engine and the tires spinning on the gravel drive indicated that Luca had left. She picked up her book, but the heroine's trials seemed paltry compared to her own. When the words blurred before her eyes for the fifth time and the tears began to fall on the page, she put the book away. She rang Olivia in the Caribbean and cried figuratively on her friend's shoulder.

• • •

Luca held back a sigh as Sophia typed away on her computer at the desk he'd set up for her in his home office. He couldn't deny she seemed happier. She'd found a purpose and was enjoying herself. When he'd discovered she was setting up her own business, he'd reacted in sheer frustration that she'd erected another wall in life without him—a life where he was only a peripheral part.

Now she was out at client meetings or site visits, scouring junkyards and meeting with artisans, often accompanied by Isabella. The two women had become close friends, and he was happy that Sophia was adjusting to life so well in Italy. He only wished he was a bigger part of the picture.

He'd thought that once they made love, he'd regain control of his life. Instead, he'd lost even more. He was obsessed, and it didn't sit well with him. He was too distracted. What he needed was a challenge, something that would take all his business acumen and construction skills to pull off—the hotel project near Teramo. He'd been in negotiations with Chet Wilkins for weeks now and they were finally ready to proceed with a site visit. But he needed Sophia to come with him to stop Chet's wife, Leslie, from swinging a wrecking ball through his plans.

"Sophia, are you still available to come to Teramo with me and the Wilkinses on Friday?"

She flicked to her calendar. "Thanks for reminding me, I almost forgot. Yes, I can adjust the meetings I have; they're not that important. How long will we be gone?" She was scheduling him into her life, like a client. He crushed the urge to walk over to her desk and pull her into his arms. To kiss her until he was all she could think about.

"Just for the weekend. This is the first site visit. If it goes well, we may have to go back again later in the week."

"Oh, next week might be a problem. But I'll deal with that if it happens. Do you really think he'll go for the place?"

"I hope so. He is deciding between Teramo and a site he saw in Spain. There are more buildings in

Teramo, but they are in worse condition. I need this contract, Sophia. It's worth twenty-five million Euros in profit to my company. Plus Chet has offered a ten percent share in the hotel. It will continue to pay, even after the work is all done. And if successful, it will make me one of the biggest property restoration companies in Italy. The name Castellioni will be known everywhere."

"Wow, I didn't realize it was such a big deal. I'm sure Chet will love Teramo. The photos you showed me were beautiful. But have you figured out how you're going to make it work if you do win the bid? How can you oversee a project six hours from here?"

He took a deep breath before delivering the bad news. "We will have to move there for at least the start of the rebuild. I have found a nice house nearby we could rent. It is not as large as this, but it will be comfortable. Once things are running smoothly I can probably appoint someone to take over. But Chet was adamant that I be personally involved."

"Luca, I just started my own business. I can't move to Teramo for an indefinite period now. I have clients. And I convinced Isabella to do this with me. I can't leave her in the lurch. You're not the only one with responsibilities."

A crushing weight descended on his chest. He pulled in a deep breath, hoping to relieve the pressure. "Come for the weekend. We can discuss the problems if I get the job." He tried to inject a note of confidence in his voice. But the excitement of negotiating what could be the biggest contract yet for his company was tainted by the thought that it might mean a separation from

Sophia. It was his worst fear, having to choose between his business and his wife.

• • •

Sophia zipped the suitcase closed and took one more look around the bedroom to make sure she hadn't forgotten anything. Usually she loved these little impromptu trips with Luca. Generally it was just a day away, occasionally an overnight stay if it was a weekend. Then he'd find a gorgeous little hotel and he'd wine and dine her, shower her with romance, until she forgot he didn't love her.

This trip, however, there would be no romance. Just a lead ball in her stomach as she contemplated weeks apart from Luca. It was the proverbial no-win situation. She could be a bitch and probably cost him the job. Or she could be super sweet and he'd win the contract and she'd lose a husband.

"Are you ready?"

Was she? "Yes, of course."

Luca yanked her case off the bed and headed out the door. He hadn't touched her. Normally, when he came near her, he would at least drop a kiss on her temple or run his hand down her arm. Some indication of wanting her, needing her. This time, nothing. Was it worry over securing the deal and the impact on their marriage? Or was he tiring of her already?

She followed him from the room and slid her sunglasses on her nose as she exited the house so he couldn't see the dampness in her eyes. He sat behind the wheel in the Land Rover, waiting for her. As soon as she climbed in, he started the vehicle and sped off with a spurt of gravel. Within minutes they were on the motorway, the beautiful Italian countryside whizzing by the window.

"Where are we meeting the Wilkinses?" she asked as the silence in the vehicle became unbearable.

"In Teramo, at the hotel. Tomorrow we will go out to the site. Did you pack your walking boots? The terrain is pretty rough."

"Yes."

Luca had been to the site earlier in the week to double check some measurements and see the access roads for himself. He'd stayed overnight, their first night apart since they'd become lovers. If he secured this deal, it wouldn't be their last.

"And you will play the loving wife so Mrs. Wilkins keeps her hands off me?"

It stung that he asked. *No, I'm going to stand back and let her have you on the reception desk.*

"It would be a disaster if the deal fell apart because Chet Wilkins cannot control his wife," Luca continued.

Like you can control yours?

"I have played the devoted wife at every business function you've taken me to, in front of our friends and your mother. I'm pretty sure I can manage to convince a lush for one weekend that I'm desperately in love with my husband."

His knuckles showed white on the steering wheel, but he didn't make any other reply.

Eight hours later, Sophia nearly kissed the ground

as Luca pulled to stop in front of a generic cement building. A couple of flags over the portico and a nondescript sign at the front were the only indications it was a hotel. The long drive from the villa had been interminable. Only once had Luca asked if she needed to stop for a break. Sensing his need to get the journey over with, she'd declined.

Traffic had been horrific. With the beautiful weather, it seemed most Italian city-dwellers were heading out to the countryside for some fresh air. At one point, they'd crawled along the motorway, rarely going above thirty miles an hour. The whole trip had emphasized just how far away it was from their home. If Luca moved here and she stayed in the villa, they'd have thirty-six hours together, if they were lucky, on the weekends. And she'd overheard a conversation where Luca had mentioned that Chet wanted the restoration done as soon as possible and was willing to pay extra for weekend work.

Which meant Luca wouldn't be able to leave. She'd have to come down and see him. And if he was busy working, what would be the point? They'd be back to the first days of their marriage when they were roommates who worked opposing shifts.

At the reception desk, Luca asked if the Wilkinses had checked in already and was told they'd arrived a half hour earlier. Before they could even make their way to the lift, Leslie Wilkins emerged from the hotel bar, drink in hand.

"There you are, darlings. Hurry up and put your bags away and meet us in the bar," Leslie said, her words only slightly slurred.

Luca slid his hand into Sophia's, the first time he'd touched her that day. "Of course, Leslie. We will just freshen up and join you in a few minutes."

Sophia swallowed down the bile that rose in her throat. It was show time. She wasn't sure why it felt different this time, pretending to be in love with Luca. Peeking at him from the corner of her eye as they rode the lift up to their third floor room, it hit her. It was no longer a pretense. She loved her husband.

Bollocks. That wasn't supposed to have happened.

• • •

Luca put his arm around Sophia and although she smiled up at him, it didn't reach her eyes. She'd been distant, more reserved around him, since he'd reminded her of the trip to Teramo earlier in the week. She was still a passionate and enthusiastic lover. But the little touches, the moments of intense connection were gone. She was withdrawing from him, millimeter by millimeter.

Chet Wilkins droned on about the boutique hotel industry. Luca had never known a man who only had one topic of conversation. He'd tried to steer the discussion to something more general where everyone could contribute. But Chet always found a way to return to his beloved niche market.

Sophia shifted in her chair next to him, and her smile became a little more forced. Her acting talent was slipping. He should be annoyed, but he'd rather have her genuine than pretending. He fiddled with a lock of her silky hair. Across from him, Leslie Wilkins was on her fourth drink, and he had to keep moving his legs under his chair to stop her rubbing her foot along his calf. The woman knew no bounds. The wives of all his other business associates had stopped making advances when he'd introduced Sophia to them. Leslie hadn't taken the hint.

"It has been a long day and we have a full schedule tomorrow. Shall we meet at seven in the restaurant?" Luca suggested.

Leslie groaned. "Darling, I don't get out of bed at seven for any man. Even one as gorgeous as you. Nine o'clock is the earliest I appear," she said.

No wonder this site visit had already been delayed by four weeks. And if they didn't start until after nine, there was no way they'd be done in one day. Luca had hoped to take Sophia to the coast before they headed back to Milan. Spend a little time with her away from both their businesses.

"If we don't start until nine, then it will be a very long day," he said.

"Then we'll just have to take two days, won't we, darling?" Leslie replied.

He stifled a groan. If this wasn't the deal of a lifetime, he'd walk out the door right now. As if sensing his frustration, Sophia put a hand on his thigh.

"Actually, I'm getting a headache. A later start is probably a good idea. If you'll excuse me, I need to take some tablets and get my head on a pillow." Sophia stood and Luca prepared to depart as well.

"You don't need to go, too, darling. Stay and have

another drink," Leslie interrupted.

Luca's eyes flashed to Chet. The man sat there like a dead fish, staring blankly into the distance. What had happened to these two that they were so indifferent to each other's needs? Had they ever been in love? Luca turned back to Sophia, who hovered by her chair. She seemed to be battling her need to flee and her promise to help him. His stomach fluttered.

"No, I will say goodnight, too. If I massage my wife's neck, sometimes her headache disappears. And we need you fresh for tomorrow, yes, *amore*?"

"Yes," she replied, her voice subdued.

As they returned to their hotel room, Sophia didn't say a word. However, as the door clicked closed behind her, she released a weary sigh.

"If I have to spend the whole day with that woman tomorrow, I may take up drinking as well," she said.

"As long as you don't take up flirting with other men."

"Why would I, when I have you? Well sort of."

"What do you mean, 'well sort of'?" He pulled her against him, cradling her head against his chest. The embrace was more for his sake than hers. He needed to feel her, know that at least the distance between them wasn't physical. Although it soon may well be.

"I mean I have that bit of you that is not married to your company."

"You have more of me than that," he whispered into her hair.

He hoped his surprise tomorrow would do the trick in convincing her to choose him over her career.

Chapter Thirteen

"Do you mind if we sit down for a bit, darling? The men can clamber all over these broken down buildings. I just want to relax and enjoy the sunshine." Leslie plonked down on a stone wall and pulled the bottle of water from her bag, taking a long swig.

Sophia waved at Luca, indicating he should go ahead with Chet. Despite having seen the photos, the village was larger than she expected and more dilapidated. There wasn't a building left with a roof, and she worried if she leaned against a wall it would collapse on her.

When they'd first arrived after eleven this morning, a sudden lightness had taken over her heart. The place was a disaster—no way would Chet want to build here. After the heavy weight that had been sitting in her chest for the past week lifted, she'd bounded from the backseat of the Land Rover, ready to explore and enjoy the day.

Within half an hour, however, Chet's concerned features had turned to elation and his expressions of "this is just perfect," and "I can see it now," became more frequent. He was enthralled with the site and the vision Luca presented to him. And glancing around now, as Leslie drained her water bottle and hunted around for another, Sophia couldn't blame him. Nestled in a small valley, sunshine seemed to bounce off all sides of the village. A flock of birds, unused to human companions, called out warning messages to their loved ones. The hills were covered in wildflowers, especially red poppies. Sophia wouldn't put it past Luca not to have planted them for effect during his previous visit.

The project that would rip her and Luca apart took a giant leap closer to reality.

"We were once like you, you know." Leslie's nasally voice interrupted Sophia's musings.

"Pardon?"

"Chet and me. We were once in love like you and Luca. Now, as soon as we get back to the States, I'm going to file for divorce." Leslie tossed her plastic water bottle over the wall. Sophia made a mental note to pick it up later. This place was too beautiful to leave litter.

"What happened, if you don't mind me asking?"

The other woman gave a bitter laugh. "Life happened, darling. It always does."

Yeah, life had happened to her parents, too. But Isabella and Dante seemed to be coping. Then again, they'd only been married a few years.

"If you loved each other once, can't you get back to that point?" Sophia had never had a real high opinion of marriage. Marriage to Luca, however, had changed that. It could be wonderful, if done right. It was something worth fighting for.

"Too much water under the bridge, as they say. Or, I guess in our case, too much infidelity and empty whiskey bottles."

"Oh." Sophia wished she hadn't asked.

"Take my advice. Don't give up your dreams for

your man, and don't let him out of your sight."

"What if the two are mutually exclusive?" Sophia sat on the wall next to Leslie. The stones giving way under her now seemed the least of her worries.

"Then you're screwed. I was a lawyer, believe it or not, when we first married. I was smart, had a career, people looked up to me. Now, I'm the pitied wife of a billionaire, someone to be entertained and accommodated so they can do a deal with my husband, and completely ignored when he's not around."

"I'm sure that's not the case," she tried to placate Leslie.

"I'm not blind, darling. I see how people look at me. But you know what? It's all a goddamned show. The drinking, the flirting… I do it in the hope that my own husband will notice me. He hasn't. Not once said a word. Never said, 'Leslie, can you please stop grabbing other men's asses while I'm standing in front of you?' He can spend hours staring at a pile of rubble and see the potential. But he can't spend five minutes with me without turning on the TV or checking his phone for messages."

Sophia shaded her eyes with her hand. Luca and Chet were on the far hill, surveying the village from a height. Luca had his arms spread wide as though he was embracing the whole valley. The fluttering in her stomach increased. How could she bear not to join him here? How could she not fight for her marriage—give up her dream and follow his?

And then what will I have when he gets bored with me?

"Why did you give up your legal career?" She turned her attention back to Leslie. Silent tears were coursing down the American woman's cheeks. Sophia searched in her bag for a tissue.

"Chet travels a lot. Scouting out locations for new properties or visiting the ones he already has. I couldn't go with him as I was up to my eyeballs in work. We were always apart. One day, a trial cancelled at the last minute; the two parties reconciled or something. Anyway, with no case to present, I suddenly had a week free. So I jetted off to join my husband. I didn't tell him I was coming; it was going to be a surprise. Well, I was the one surprised as I walked in on him in bed with his personal assistant."

"I'm so sorry." It was the lamest thing to say, but she couldn't think of a more appropriate response.

"Yeah, so was he. Sorry he got caught. But Chet begged me to give him another chance. Said all the time apart was killing him. So to save my marriage I gave up my career and started following him around the world."

"Surely Chet realized the sacrifice you made to be with him."

"You'd think, but no. He's so obsessed with his blasted hotels, they're more important to him than me. Some days, I wonder if he'd even notice if I left. Do you know the last time my husband made love to me?"

"I hope that's a rhetorical question," Sophia replied.

Leslie laughed, a bitter, horrible sound that echoed off the broken walls, throwing the sound back to them in shattered waves. "No, really. I was hoping you'd remember. Because I sure as hell don't." Her gaze flicked to the two men on the hill. "But I'm guessing you don't have that problem. Yet."

No, Luca was an incredible lover. Always making sure she was satisfied first, bringing her to the edge of ecstasy time and again until she begged him to take her. He liked hearing her scream his name as she climaxed. Except last night. She thought he'd forgone the lovemaking in deference to her pretend headache. But what if it was the excitement of being so close to his precious deal that made him want to bask in that glow instead?

"Maybe you could convince him to take some time off. You two could reconnect. Talk," Sophia suggested.

"Trust me, I've tried. But there's always one more building, one more site, one more whatever. It never ends. Business is his passion."

"Are you going to go back to the law?"

"Who wants to hire a washed-up fifty-eight-year-old lawyer with a drinking problem? No, the best I can hope for is Chet settles one of his beachfront houses on me. Then I can hire a pool boy who won't mind me ogling him as he skims the palm fronds from the water."

"That doesn't sound fair."

"It's not. I gambled my career on my marriage and lost both."

Sophia leaned over the wall and threw up her breakfast.

• • •

Luca could fly down the hill. He couldn't wait to tell

Sophia. Chet had decided on Teramo and wanted construction to begin as soon as the contracts were signed. Castellioni's was going to be the biggest restoration firm in Italy. And this was just the beginning.

He slowed to keep pace with the older man.

"You have a classy wife," Chet said. It was the first personal remark Luca had heard the other man say.

"Yes, we're very happy."

"Well, I hope you can make it last. Leslie used to be classy."

There was no reply to that.

When they finally made it back to the village, Luca searched for Sophia. He'd seen her sat on a wall chatting to Leslie, but now she was nowhere to be found.

"If you're looking for Sophia, she's laying down in the truck." Leslie appeared from behind a bush, squeezing some hand sanitizer into her palm.

"Is she okay?" Luca didn't wait for the answer and jogged back to where he'd parked the Land Rover.

As he got closer he could see the passenger seat reclined, both front doors open for some cross-breeze. Her eyes were closed, her breathing soft and gentle. Another wave of warmth filled his chest. He didn't want to wake her but needed to know if she was all right.

"Sophia?" He caressed her cheek. As her green eyes fluttered open he sucked in a breath. She was so beautiful.

"Hi." Her voice sounded raw and her face was blotchy. Had she been crying?

"Are you sick? Shall I take you back to the hotel?"

"No, I'm okay. Just needed to lay down. The sun is

really powerful in the valley, and I forgot my hat."

He wasn't convinced that was all that was wrong but couldn't challenge her here. Chet and Leslie were about five meters away. "I have a surprise for you. Are you sure you are all right to keep going?"

She smiled, a faint replica of her usual full megawatt grin. His chest tightened again.

"Feeling better, darling?" Leslie's saccharine endearment made his skin crawl.

"Yes, thank you, Leslie. Luca has a surprise for us. Are you all done here?"

"Yup. It's going to be the most amazing hotel in my portfolio. Your husband is a visionary, Sophia. If this turns out half as good as he says, I see a bright future for our two companies."

Sophia swallowed at Chet's announcement. "Yes, he's brilliant. He sees the potential in things that others miss." She put the chair back into its upright position and exited the vehicle. "I can't wait to see what he has in store for us next."

She resumed her seat in the back and Chet climbed in the front. Luca tried to check on her through the rearview mirror but she kept her head turned to the side, looking out the window. He wished he hadn't arranged for the surprise now. Sophia looked like she could do with some downtime away from Leslie … and he could do with some private time with his wife.

The road grew more rutted as he drove. There was no way a regular car would make it down here. He made a mental note to order some gravel before construction got underway. After twenty minutes he finally pulled up in front of a two-story stone cottage, set against the hillside. He shut off the engine and the only sound to be heard was the trickle of a waterfall and birds singing in the trees.

"What's this?" Leslie asked.

Luca turned around in his seat to see Sophia's face. "This is the house I rented, in case Chet and I were able to come to an agreement. One of the restaurants in Teramo has prepared a meal for us. Come, this is my surprise."

Sophia stared out the windscreen at the house then did a long, slow blink. The kind of blink that said she wasn't sure what he expected her to say. After two months of marriage, he was finally learning her tells. He could almost see her acting mask slip back into place.

She got out of the Land Rover and stood beside him. Luca tried to see the cottage through her eyes. It was a bit sad looking, not having been lived in for over a year. But the gardeners and cleaners he'd hired had tidied the place nicely. The curtains and windows were clean, and the bramble had been cut back from the path. With a fresh coat of paint on the shutters and a little maintenance here and there, it would be a cozy home for the two of them.

"What do you think?" he finally asked, unable to bear her silence any longer.

"It looks charming," she said, with only a slight hitch in her voice.

"Did you say there was food? I'm starving." Leslie's voice grated down his spine.

"Yes, of course. Please follow me." Luca led them

around the side of the house to where a picnic table had been set up. A white-coated man stood at attention, sweeping away the lids covering the food as they arrived. A young woman appeared from inside the house, carrying a tray with glasses of chilled prosecco.

"I'll say one thing about you Italians, you sure know how to eat," Leslie said as she snagged a glass of the sparkling wine.

Sophia declined the wine when offered and asked for a glass of water instead.

"Are you sure you are all right?" Luca put a finger under her chin and examined her face. She was a little pale, but the smile she gave him was a bit more real.

"Yes, of course. I just don't feel like wine so early in the day," she said quietly, her eyes darting toward Leslie.

"Chet, Leslie, do you mind starting? I want to show Sophia the cottage."

"Of course, go right ahead," Chet answered. He picked up a plate and loaded it with olives, pickled mushrooms, artichoke hearts, and cheeses.

Luca took Sophia's hand in his and led her into the cottage. Sheltered by the mountain behind, it was cooler than outside. He glanced around, pleased that the place appeared neat and clean. The cottage had a rustic charm he was sure the designer in Sophia could appreciate.

"I know it is tiny compared to the villa. As it is just the two of us, I did not think we really needed a lot of room." He stared at her face, waiting for some indication of what she was thinking.

"It's very pretty. It's nice how they've kept all the

original features."

"One family has owned it for 200 years. They don't want to sell, but neither does anyone want to live here, so it is available for as long as we want."

She pulled her hand out of his and wandered over to the stone sink, running her finger along its bumpy surface in a long caress.

"If you want, I can hire a cook and gardener to come from Teramo."

She raised her eyes to his but still didn't say anything. A shimmer of dampness appeared and she quickly blinked it away. He was such an idiot. She wasn't well. He should have taken her back to the hotel, not sprung this surprise on her.

"Come upstairs, I think you will like the view from the bedroom."

He took her hand in his again and led the way up the narrow stone steps. If he carried her to bed he'd have to be very careful not to bump her head. Of course, with no one around for miles, they didn't necessarily have to wait until they made it to the bedroom to enjoy each other.

Sophia stuck her head through the doorway of the two small bedrooms. The furniture upstairs had been in such bad shape that he'd had the owner's permission to get rid of it. He figured Sophia would enjoy finding new pieces. Even though it was only a temporary home, she'd probably feel better if she could stamp some of her own personality on it, as she'd done with the villa, which now had the heart and soul it had been lacking before she'd come to live there.

"This is the master bedroom," Luca said as he flung open a door at the end of the small hallway. It had probably been two or even three rooms originally, judging by the ceiling. But at some time in the past fifty years, it had been turned into a cozy room with attached bathroom. "Come look at the claw-foot tub. I thought you would enjoy that."

"I don't know what to say," she whispered at last.

Luca pulled her into his arms, holding her tight. He rested his cheek on the top of her head and rubbed his hands up and down her back until he felt her relax.

"We'll come back tomorrow, or next week, when you're feeling better. Then we can look for some furniture, and new curtains, and anything else you think we need. I want you to be happy here, Sophia. Whatever it takes, it is yours."

She clung to him tightly for a few more minutes, and his heart rate accelerated. He'd never seen her like this. Even when she'd told him of her family and her past, she'd been more animated.

Her stomach rumbled, and he gave himself another mental kick up the ass. He was making a disaster of this husband role. "You must be starving. We can eat now and discuss all that needs to be done later."

He led her back down the stairs and out into the sunshine. Three empty glasses of wine sat on the tray, and Chet still had his next to him. What had happened to Leslie that she'd gone from classy to trashy?

"Sit here, *amore*. I'll get you a plate." He hurried over to the buffet and picked out her favorites.

She gave him a warm smile as he handed her the

plate and he managed a deep breath, the pressure in his chest releasing a little. He still hadn't shown her the cottage's best feature, and he was trying to decide whether to wait until the Wilkinses weren't with them or show them all after lunch.

Sophia picked at her food but downed three glasses of water. After everyone said they were done eating, Luca stood.

"I have one more surprise. If you do not mind a little walk after eating, follow me."

He took Sophia's hand and made sure to slow his walk so she didn't get out of breath. It was the perfect day to show her the view. They wound their way through a forested path. A small bridge spanned a creek, which tumbled over some rocks further down in a picturesque waterfall near the house. He'd make sure there was a comfortable chair there for Sophia to read in.

After about ten minutes, the trees thinned and they emerged onto a little plateau. A slate terrace and a pergola covered in roses graced the center. They all wandered over and stared at the view. In the far distance the blue Aegean Sea shimmered in the early-summer sunshine. But it was the magnificent view of the medieval village they would be turning into a world-class spa hotel that was the real prize.

"See, from here you will be able to watch as we turn the past into the future. I plan to take a photo every day when it is not raining and create a slideshow of our progress."

"What a great idea," Chet said. "It will make great marketing material."

"The view is beautiful," Sophia agreed.

Leslie huffed. "I'm sure Rapunzel said the same thing when she looked out of her tower."

Chapter Fourteen

Sophia leaned her head against the cool tile wall of the hotel bathroom, hoping to quell the rising nausea. Luca and Chet had gone to a meeting with the regional planning committee to discuss the restoration of the village and its transformation into a hotel complex. They didn't expect any opposition to their plans as the tax revenue and local employment benefits were substantial. Leslie had pleaded a headache and decided to stay in the hotel, so Sophia had been relieved of her chaperone duties.

Now she could vomit in peace, without Luca hovering over her. He'd been really sweet at the cottage, almost carrying her down the hill in the end. And for the drive back to Teramo, he'd insisted that she sit up front with him, relegating the billionaire Chet to the backseat, next to his wife.

Sophia had pretended to sleep while Luca and Chet discussed the initial construction phase. They were going to start with the smallest houses, which were to serve as accommodation for the workers while they rebuilt the larger structures. She and Luca were to live at the cottage for at least the first year, although Chet acknowledged that Luca had other projects that would require his attention so he didn't need to be onsite every day. Luca already had someone who would take over from him in Milan, dealing with the day-to-day business aspects of his company.

Next they talked about other places in Italy and southern France where they could possibly replicate the project. At that point, Sophia stopped listening. Leslie was right. There was always one more deal.

Her mother's pinched face loomed before her mind. The disillusion, the drudgery, the despair of giving up on her dreams had haunted Janice Stevens until there was no light left within her to shine on her children. Sophia couldn't, wouldn't let that happen to her. But could she really be so selfish as to pursue her dream at the cost of Luca's? Isabella had said that she put her husband's happiness before her own, knowing that he did the same. If it was always the one person giving up their happiness, however, could the marriage last? And would Luca soon lose interest in her, as Chet had done with Leslie, if she had nothing to bring to the relationship?

The turmoil of her thoughts echoed in her stomach.

Her mobile phone rang in the other room and she hurried to answer it, although if it was Luca, she wasn't sure that she wanted to speak to him just yet.

"*Ciao*, Isabella," Sophia said, seeing her friend's name on the call display.

"Sophia, I have the great news. But first, did Luca get the job?"

"Yes. He is meeting with the officials now to get started on the paperwork."

"You do not sound happy." Trust Isabella to pick up on that hundreds of kilometers away when her husband hadn't been able to work it out while standing in the same tiny room in a cottage.

"It means Luca has to move down here for at least a year, probably two." Sophia's stomach roiled again and she took a drink of water.

"Oh, I see. Then that makes my news of no matter."

"What's your news?"

"You remember my friend from school who works with a company that rents houses to English tourists?"

"Yes, we met her at lunch a few days ago."

"Well, her company is looking to redecorate all twenty of their properties. They want to combine local Italian features with some English style so the guests will feel more at home. She wants us to bid on the contract. She believes you will be a top contender to be the chief designer as you know both cultures. But if you will not be living in the area…" The excitement in Isabella's voice faded away.

"How much is the contract worth?" she swallowed again.

"Fifty thousand euros. And that would be just our commission. The total budget for the redecoration is 200,000." Her dream come true. Dare she take it?

"I'll have to call you back, Isabella. I think I'm going to be sick." Sophia raced to the bathroom, making it just in time.

• • •

Luca stared down at Sophia curled in the fetal position on the bed. His heart swelled and it was time he admitted it, at least to himself. He was in love with his wife.

Sophia had become the foundation that supported the rest of his life. When he was with her, he experienced an inner peace he hadn't even realized was missing. The sense of purpose he'd been unconsciously searching for, he'd found in her arms. His money, his success, it all meant nothing if she wasn't there to share it.

He wanted to tell her. But, his head told him to hold back. Sophia was always so serene, so in control. He had no idea what she really felt. Sometimes, she even appeared to be playing a role. On the drive down from Milan, she said she could easily fool Leslie that she was desperately in love with her husband. What he would give to make it real. This deal? The future of his company? His stomach felt like it was falling.

He sighed. This wasn't supposed to be so complicated. Sophia seemed to enjoy his company, she certainly enjoyed their lovemaking. Was he still just her ticket to an easier life? She never asked him to stay home or made any demands of him. He couldn't give her his heart if she didn't want it.

He would have to be content with telling her how he felt during the heat of their passion. Of course he had to tell her in his mother's native language, as Sophia's Italian was too good now for her not to know what he was saying. The wry thought passed through his mind that his mother would be so proud that he could still remember some of the Sardinian she'd taught him as a child.

As he continued to stare, her eyes fluttered open and she stretched.

"What time is it?" Her voice was husky with sleep.

"Almost eleven. Sorry to be so late. We went for drinks after our meeting to celebrate. Have you eaten?" He glanced around the room. There were no room service dishes here or in the hallway outside the room.

"No, something I had at breakfast didn't agree with me. I haven't felt like eating."

He sat on the bed beside her and checked her forehead for a fever. If anything, she was a little cool. "I think we should take you to a doctor."

"Honestly, Luca, you worry too much. I'll be fine in the morning. What's the schedule for tomorrow? Are we going back to the site?"

"No, there's no need. I may still have to go back next week if the regional planners have any questions. I thought tomorrow we would take the coastal road back, stop in some of the villages, and enjoy the sea air."

"Actually, I would like to get back to the villa as soon as possible tomorrow. Isabella and I have an important meeting on Monday and I'd like to prepare. We have a chance to bid on a huge contract to redecorate twenty rental properties."

There was a sharp stabbing pain in his chest. "Twenty? That is amazing."

She yawned again. "Are you coming to bed now?"

He searched her face, her eyes were already closed.

"Actually, I have a few emails to send first. I'll join you in a little while."

"Okay, 'night."

He turned away from the bed and grabbed his laptop out of his bag. He'd work in the lobby so as not to disturb her. The chances were slim that he'd actually be able to concentrate and send the urgent messages. Not when the distinct possibility of living apart from his wife loomed large before him. But he had seventy-five people depending on him for work—he couldn't just pack it in because he wanted to spend every possible moment with Sophia.

He couldn't give up the hotel project and he couldn't take it.

• • •

Sophia stepped through the door to the villa. She loved this house. Would she love it the same if Luca weren't living here? Probably not.

At least she felt better than yesterday. A good night's sleep and a couple cups of tea had done the trick. That, and leaving Teramo in the rearview mirror. But that respite was probably short-lived.

Maria bustled out of the kitchen as Luca brought in their bags, informing them that dinner would be ready in about an hour.

"Do you need to work on the proposal for your meeting tomorrow?" There was an odd light in Luca's eyes. Probably the same look she got when he talked about his project.

"No. Isabella is coming over tomorrow morning, and we'll work on it together then."

"Shall we take a walk in the garden?"

She searched his eyes and saw hope and something else. Fear? "I'd love that."

He took her hand and they strolled toward the

rotunda set in the topiary garden. The trailing roses were in full bloom and their delicate scent filled the air with perfume.

"You don't like the cottage, do you?" Luca stopped walking and tilted her face up, his thumb gently caressing her cheek.

"The cottage is fine. It's just so far from anywhere. I'll be trapped there while you're at work."

"It is only for a little while. There is no other option, Sophia. The city is more than two hours away. We plan to start construction at 6:00 a.m. If we live in town I will have to leave by four and will not get home until after eight at night."

"I know." She tried to blink it away, but a tear fell down her cheek. Luca bent and kissed it away, holding her close.

"I cannot bear for us to live apart, *amore*. It hurts to even think about it."

"For me, too. But I'm scared of what I will become. I told you when we first married that I didn't do sitting around the house well. And what if you tire of me? You will be dealing with interesting people all day, and when you come home the only thing I'll be able to talk about is the dust bunny I chased around the sitting room."

"Dust bunny?"

"Never mind. The point is, I'll be bored out of my mind. What if I turn into Leslie Wilkins?"

"You will never become that. You are too strong. You are my warrior ninja woman. And I don't know why you think I'll get tired of you. You fascinate me, Sophia. More each day." He kissed her lips, absorbing her sigh.

Yeah, but for how long?

• • •

Sophia shut down her laptop and prepared to answer questions. Thankfully she was sitting and they couldn't see how badly her knees were shaking. Even Isabella, who always seemed so confident, was fiddling with their paper proposal in front of her. The board had been silent during her presentation, and Sophia had no idea whether she'd nailed it or missed by a mile.

"Thank you, Signora Castellioni and Signora Carrero. That is the best presentation we have seen. You understood exactly what we were looking for," the chairman said. The elation Sophia expected to feel was squashed by her nausea. "Do any of the other board members have questions?" John Templeton looked around the room. An ex-British Army commander, he was as rigid as a concrete wall. No one, it seemed, dared question him. "Very well, then. We will make a decision this evening and let you know the results."

Sophia and Isabella managed to wait until they were in Isabella's car before they shouted in glee. Isabella pulled out her mobile and called Dante. Sophia couldn't understand the conversation—it was too fast in Italian—but she could hear the pride in Dante's voice as he congratulated his wife. Sophia's fingers hovered over the screen of her phone. Should she call Luca?

He'd done his best to be supportive, but she knew his heart wasn't in it. When they'd made love for the past three nights, each was as if it were the last time. There was a poignancy in his kisses that had never been there before.

Her phone buzzed in her hand. Luca calling. Was he excited to hear how her presentation went? Or was he hoping she'd failed?

"*Amore*, where are you?"

"I'm in Monza. I've just finished my presentation."

"Have you forgot that we're to have dinner with one of my clients tonight?"

Damn, in her excitement she had forgotten. "No. Sorry, I'll be home in a few minutes. The people before us went over their allotted time, so we are running a little late."

"I'll wait for you. Please do not be long." No question about how it went.

"He is not happy?" Isabella turned her astute eyes on Sophia.

"No."

"If they offer us the contract, we do not have to accept," Isabella reasoned.

"I know. Will you hate me if I say 'no'?"

"Never. You must decide what is more important to you, your career or your marriage. It is not a decision I would like to make."

"But didn't you give up your career as a journalist for your marriage?"

"No, not really. It did not make me as happy as being with Dante. But I see your face when you talk about design. You are very excited and you make everyone else excited too."

Design did make her happy. But happier than she

was with Luca?

Isabella started the car and drove Sophia home.

Luca was pacing the front hallway when she arrived. There was a grim line around his mouth, and he skipped their usual hello kiss.

"I'll change quickly and be right down," Sophia promised.

The dinner was so boring, Sophia had to restrain herself from checking her watch. The client's wife had narrowed her eyes when Luca had introduced her but still managed to take every opportunity to put her hand on Luca's arm and laugh provocatively at anything Luca said that was even remotely funny. Sophia alternated between wanting to rip the other woman's arm off and spill red wine on her white silk dress. She really should have taken up ninja training. Then she could have dispatched her with grace and stealth.

That brought a smile to her lips. Luca leaned over and whispered in her ear, "I'm pleased to see you happy again. It's been too long."

She squeezed his hand where it rested on the table. He lifted their joined hands and kissed the back of hers, oblivious to the couple sat opposite them. The woman glared at her again, but Sophia didn't care. Luca was hers.

"Don't let him out of your sight." Leslie's dire warning flitted through her brain.

Thirty minutes later they sat in the Maserati. When Luca didn't start the engine, she turned to him.

"Thank you for coming with me tonight. I know you're tired and would have preferred to stay at home.

Are you still ill from Teramo? You look a little pale." He cupped her cheek, his thumb rubbed lightly across her lips.

She pressed a kiss against his thumb and he smiled. "I think it's just because I've been inside so much lately. A few days in the garden and I'll look better."

"Hmm." He didn't look convinced. Before he could question her further, both their mobile phones buzzed. Their peripherals were more in synch than they were.

"*Mi scusi*. The planning committee in Teramo held a special meeting tonight on the project. They said they would let me know their decision."

While he read his message, Sophia glanced at hers. There were several missed calls from her brother and an email from the property rental company. They offered her the contract and wanted her to begin in ten days.

"All is approved. We can start in two weeks," he said, triumph in his voice. "Let's go home and celebrate."

• • •

Several hours later, a thoroughly satisfied Sophia curled up against Luca. His heartbeat was steady under her ear, his warmth enveloped her. Although she was still slightly embarrassed at her loud reactions to their lovemaking, she couldn't deny the effect he had on her. "I like the way you celebrate."

"Glad to hear it—almost as much as I like hearing your expressions of contentment." She could hear the self-satisfied grin in his voice.

"Hmm," she ran her hand up his thigh and felt his instant reaction. "I seem to recall a rather vocal response from you as well."

"Really?" He rolled her onto her back, his hand sliding up from her hip to her breast. "I don't think I said anything. Perhaps we'd better test this theory of yours," he whispered against her lips, before taking them in a blistering kiss.

He was trailing his lips down her throat when the jarring sound of the phone ringing made him raise his head. "This is very bad timing. Must be my mother. Should I tell her she'll never become a *nonna* if she telephones when we're in bed?" He rolled away and picked up the receiver.

Still in a fog of bliss, it took a moment for her to understand the voice on the other end, asking if this was the correct number for her.

"Yes, she's here. Who is calling?"

"It's your brother, James," Luca said, passing over the phone.

"Hello, James." She cleared her throat, which was still raspy with desire. "What's wrong? You usually call me on my mobile phone."

"I tried your mobile all evening. You never answered my calls or messages. Finally I got in touch with your friend Olivia, who gave me this number. Who answered the phone?" Her brother sounded upset but curious to find a man answering his sister's home number.

"That was Luca, my husband." She moved the phone away from her ear as James's "what?" echoed through the room. "I'll tell you all about it later. What's so urgent you are calling so late?" She sat up, clutching the sheet to her chest.

"It's Mum. She's taken a bad turn and is in hospital. Sophia, the doctors don't think she is going to last much longer. They say she has only a day or two left. She wants to see you one last time." James's voice cracked with emotion.

"Oh, James! I thought she was doing better. I'll catch the first flight in the morning... No, no, I'll meet you at the hospital. I take it she's at North Mid?" Her voice was calm, but her hands shook. She spoke with James a couple more minutes before hanging up the phone.

She glanced at Luca and her heart flipped. How could she decide between her husband and her dream? Her future was such a disaster, she might as well go back to the past.

Chapter Fifteen

Luca had already gotten out of bed and was standing next to it, wearing his dressing gown, holding hers out for her to slip into.

"I am coming with you," he said firmly.

She gazed up at her husband and saw compassion, and something else she couldn't identify on his face. "Luca, I would love for you to come. But I don't think this is the most appropriate time for you to meet my family. If my mum really is dying, then finding out in her last hours that I'm married will only upset her. I can't tell her our marriage is a business arrangement; she wouldn't understand. All she'll think is that her oldest daughter didn't even invite her to the wedding. And it will remind her of how crappy a mother she'd been to me. I'd rather she went to her grave in peace."

A flicker of pain crossed Luca's eyes, and his hand flew to his chest as though she'd stabbed him in the heart. Then he blinked and the expression disappeared, although he still looked ready to argue with her. "Can we compromise and you come out for the funeral? You can meet my father and the rest of my family then. Also, if the doctors are wrong and she lives longer, you won't have to fly back and forth. Don't you need to sign a bunch of contracts for the hotel project this week?"

"I told you that you would never have to cope alone

again, and I meant it." He paused, as if considering her arguments. "Okay. I will wait for your call. But I am serious, call at any time and for any reason, and I will be on the next plane." He took the clothes out of her hands that she'd been picking up from the floor. He tossed them on the sofa across the room and pulled her against him.

"Thank you," she mumbled into his chest. She didn't want to leave his warm embrace. Her career might provide her with some financial security and personal satisfaction. But it couldn't compete with the haven of his arms, or the bliss that filled her when he smiled at her.

"Pack a bag and I will book you a seat on the first plane in the morning." Luca leaned back and seemed to search her face. She could feel the walls build up inside of her again as she prepared to face her family.

With an enigmatic shake of his head, he finally let her go to make the necessary arrangements. She listened to the messages on her mobile phone—several from James and one from Olivia telling her that she had given James her home number and asking her to call back no matter what the time.

• • •

Leaden skies greeted her arrival back in England. The early morning sunshine in Italy seemed a lifetime away. This stormy weather, however, reflected her state of mind. Automatically, she scanned the crowd waiting for arriving passengers. Warmth filled her as she caught sight of a familiar face. She hadn't anticipated how happy she would be that Olivia hadn't listened to her about not coming to the airport.

"I saw a uniformed man holding a card with your name on it. Did your gorgeous husband arrange a car for you?" Olivia said, after embracing her.

"Probably. He made all the arrangements last night while I packed. Luca wanted to come, but I managed to convince him that now wasn't the best time to spring a husband on my family."

"No, I guess not. But you're going to have to tell them soon. I don't think it will be too long before you have a gaggle of children following you."

"What do you mean?" Sophia could feel the heat creep up her neck.

Olivia laughed. "You no longer have that gaunt, haunted look, as if waiting for the final blow to do you in. You now look healthy, radiant even. Like a flower that has at long last been moved into the sunshine. Marriage suits you. I've never seen you look better."

"You should try it. You look exhausted. Are you still burning the candle at both ends?" She noted the dark circles under Olivia's eyes that her friend had unsuccessfully tried to conceal.

"No. I broke it off with Stuart. I realized he only wanted me for my looks. When we would go out he would show me off to his friends, but at home he just ignored me. He wasn't interested in what I wanted or needed. He was like all the others. That's it. I'm off men for good."

"Oh, Livy, I seriously doubt that. You have too

much love to give to go solo for the rest of your life. The right man is out there, you just need to be a bit more … selective."

"Well, one thing is for certain. I'm going to take a leaf out of your book, and I'm not jumping into bed with another man until there's a ring on my finger—preferably a wedding ring. Then I'll know it's serious."

The drive to the hospital was accomplished in near silence. Sophia's thoughts alternated between the bleak reunion that awaited her, and the ever-constant worry about her and Luca's conflicting careers. If someone had told her four months ago that she'd be sitting in the back of a luxury car, trying to decide whether to accept a 50,000 euro contract or join her gorgeous and kind Italian millionaire husband living in one of the most beautiful parts of the world she'd ever seen, she'd have laughed.

Before she'd resolved her dilemma, they arrived at the hospital. As they walked into the building, both women wrinkled their noses and shivered. They put their arms around each other at the shared memory of fleeing the hospital together in the middle of the night.

"Give me your bag. I'll be in the waiting room down the hall." Olivia said as they stood outside the room number James had given last night on the phone.

"It's not really necessary…" Sophia began.

"It is necessary. Don't be a bore and argue. I have a delightful book to read, another one of your habits I've taken up … and handsome doctors to ogle."

"That sounds more like you. Sworn off men, my foot."

Olivia hugged her, then took her bag before gliding down the hall. Sophia took a deep breath, opened the door to the room, and stepped inside. Her mother lay in the bed, eyes closed, exceedingly pale, her skin almost transparent. Her father sat in a hard plastic chair, holding his wife's hand, his head bent as he slept. Although his face was relaxed, he looked drained, as though his life, too, was ebbing away.

She took a moment to study her parents, relieved to find that, despite the turbulent past, she was able to look at them without animosity. Luca's support and the new life she had in Italy made this possible.

Walking over to the bed, she took her mother's other hand. Janice opened her eyes and Sophia could see the dark shadows, and the pain she couldn't hide. It took a moment for her mother to focus and recognize her daughter.

"Sophia! Is that really you? You look so different, so beautiful. Thank you for coming." Her voice was barely a whisper but it woke her father, who stared at her.

"Of course I came. You are my mother." Her voice cracked at seeing her mother so frail. What she wouldn't give to have Luca's arms around her right now.

"James said you're living in Italy now, that you have a good job there," her dad put in. She'd begged James not to mention her marriage; it was something she had to tell her parents herself. Thankfully her brother had lived up to his promise.

"Yes, I live in a lovely house near Milan with a beautiful garden. When you're better, Mum, you'll have to come over. Sitting in the garden with the warm sun on your face will do you a world of good." She tried to keep a positive tone, despite having to speak past a lump in her throat.

Her mother just smiled and her father looked out the window at the grey skies. A few drops of rain slid down the glass like tears.

"Where is James? I expected him to be here." She looked around the small room, a few cards from friends on the bedside table, and some dying blooms on the window ledge the only decoration in the sterile environment. Repressing a shudder at the coldness of the room, she reinforced her smile for her parents' sake.

"He went to get some breakfast. He should be back shortly. Sarah will probably be here in an hour or so. She has to wait for a babysitter." Her father's voice was raspy as if he was trying to hold back tears.

Before the silence became unbearable, James entered the room and swept her into a big hug, lifting her completely off the floor. After he put her down, she scrutinized her brother. Even though it was only six months since she'd last seen him, he seemed to have changed from boy to man in that time. He was as tall as Luca but fair where her husband was dark. Her parents were frail and weak. James was strong and vibrant.

"Sophia, you look fabulous. I could almost say you're glowing." He held her at arm's length, studying her carefully.

"It's the Italian sunshine. I spend a lot of time outside in the garden. I passed my interior design course so I'm doing that now." James looked like he was about to question the real reason for his sister's transformation, but after her warning glare, he shrugged.

"Well, whatever it is, it suits you. How are you feeling today, Mum?" He shifted the attention back to Janice.

"Not bad. The nurse gave me some more morphine about an hour ago. Come sit next to me, Sophia, and tell me all about Italy." She sat on the bed and held her mother's hand, pleased to find her grip was still strong. She talked about her life in Italy, playing up the interior design work she was doing, avoiding any mention of her marriage. It was hard not to talk about Luca, the center of her world. But she could tell that surprising her mother with that news would be too much for her to bear.

Sarah arrived an hour or so later. Although they shared the same coloring and physique, Sarah always had a look of vulnerability that clearly distinguished the two sisters. Sarah twirled a lock of her hair, like she used to do as a child, even though she was a mother herself. The family talked about everything and nothing, pretending it was a normal reunion and that one of them wasn't fading away before their eyes.

"I think Mum needs some rest now." She noticed her mother's grip had significantly weakened. She was exhausted as well, not having slept the night before.

"James, will you stay with your mum while I take Sophia to the flat? Sarah probably has to get back to the children now, too." Her father stood up, unfolding his tall frame with effort. Sophia was shocked at how old he appeared.

"Sleep well, Mum. I'll be back to see you in a few

hours." She kissed her mother on the cheek. Her heart tugged as she couldn't remember the last time she'd done that.

They collected Olivia from the waiting room before heading back to the flat. Sarah went off to her own home to look after her children. Standing in front of the building she had grown up in, Sophia suppressed a shudder. She wished Luca was there with her to dispel the bad memories—to put his arms around her and give her strength. Right now it didn't matter whether he loved her or not. She needed him, unconditionally.

"Dad, why don't you go up? I'm going to show Olivia where the station is." She really wanted to phone Luca but didn't think now was the time to tell her father about him. Charlie looked like he was about to collapse under the weight of his grief, and she waited till he entered the building before walking with Olivia around the corner.

"I'll come by the hospital tomorrow after work," Olivia said, hugging her. "Unless you call me first. Are you sure you want to stay here? You can sleep at my place."

"I'd better stay here. My dad needs me. James is going to do the overnight shift at the hospital tonight so Dad will be all alone. I'm going to call Luca and then I'll go in. See you tomorrow. Oh, and Olivia, you are the best." Sophia knew she didn't need to say anything else.

"I'm only a phone call away." They hugged again and then Olivia strode off in the direction of the station.

Sophia phoned Luca, closing her eyes as he answered, so his deep voice could envelope her. "I'll call you as soon as … well, I'll call you if the situation changes. Otherwise I'll speak with you again tomorrow evening," she finished off. She wanted to end the call saying "I love you," but it wouldn't be right to say it for the first time over the phone.

If there was one thing seeing her mother dying had taught her, it was that life was too short not to tell the important people in your life how you felt. Even if it was something they thought they didn't want. As soon as she got back to Italy, she was going to tell Luca she loved him.

She pulled and then pushed the front door of the building rather than buzz up to the flat. Seven years and the council still hadn't fixed the major flaw in the security. With each step she recited the name of a flower in Italian, trying to hold back the memories. The flat door was unlocked, and she closed her eyes and took a deep breath as she stepped across the threshold. She hadn't been inside since the morning she'd left for school and never came home.

The flat was an absolute tip. Used dishes covered every level surface. Clothes were piled haphazardly, making it impossible to tell the dirty from the clean. She changed into jeans and a t-shirt and set about getting the place sorted. At least she wouldn't have too much time to think if she were busy.

Her father looked up once or twice as she moved around the room, gathering the plates and endless cups of half-drunk tea. There wasn't much in the fridge, but using her newly learned cooking skills, she managed to put together a decent meal.

"Thanks." Her father looked surprised at the plate she handed to him. "Wow, this looks and smells really good." He ate hungrily. "I've been living on hospital food and canned beans for the past week."

They finished the meal in silence, and she went back to setting the flat in order. At six o'clock they made a brief visit to the hospital to relieve James while he went to get something to eat. Janice never woke up while they were there.

"They had to up her morphine to deal with the pain," James informed them on his return. "The doctor said she would probably be unconscious most of the time now."

"Call us if she wakes and wants to see us," Sophia said as they left, giving James a hug. He looked so despondent, the way she'd felt for months after Ben had died.

She returned to the flat with her father and finished the cleaning. Her whole body ached from the effort to fight off the memories. But it didn't compare with the pain of missing Luca. She tossed and turned for an hour before finally falling into a disturbed sleep in her old bed.

• • •

Sophia woke early the next morning, and after a quick breakfast of tea and toast made her way to the hospital. She'd left a note for her father telling him where she'd gone. He'd looked so tired the night before, she didn't have the heart to wake him. Besides, she could use a little time on her own.

"James, why don't you go home and get some proper rest? I'll sit with her now."

James looked up bleary eyed at her and nodded his assent. "She hasn't woken up. Call if there's any change. I'll be back in a few hours."

She sat beside her dying mother, holding her hand. It was hard to equate the frail woman in the bed with her memories. Although her mother had been a mere shadow in her life, she'd always been a vivacious, beautiful woman and that was how Sophia tried to remember her.

If it were Sophia lying in the bed, her last hours ebbing away, how would she want to be remembered? As a great interior designer, having made homes stylish across northern Italy? Or as a wonderful wife, a loving mother, the nucleus who held a family together? The answer was obvious.

It was almost noon before the rest of the family arrived, en masse. Her father appeared more rested and was freshly shaven. Sarah still looked on the verge of tears, but managed a watery smile for Sophia.

"Sorry it took me so long. I had to wait for my boyfriend to come and look after the children. He's a policeman and was on night shift," Sarah added, almost triumphantly.

"How did you meet a policeman?" James had told her that Sarah finally had a decent boyfriend, and she was interested to learn more about him.

"His name is Andrew, and he came to arrest my previous boyfriend, baby Rose's father. Andrew was so sweet. He came back the next day to see if I was okay, and the day after that. When he had his first day off, he came and took the children to the park with me. He loves them and they love him. And before you ask, we're not living together. He says I've had enough men treat me badly; he wants to show me what a gentleman is like."

"He sounds wonderful. I look forward to meeting him," Sophia said, genuinely pleased for her sister. In some ways, Sarah was the stronger one. Despite all the disappointments and heartbreaks, her sister had never lost faith in love. Maybe it was time Sophia trusted it, too.

Before she worked out how to get her business-first husband to love her, the hospital room door was thrust aside and two huge men strode into the room. It took a moment for Sophia to recognize the first one as her brother, Paul. His blonde hair was cut so short he looked bald, and his blue eyes were hard and filled with hate. He scanned the room as if looking for a fight. Catching sight of her, his face softened. When he smiled, she saw a hint of her brother as he'd been, before.

The other man checked out the room and its occupants, looking out the window and into the small attached toilet. He appeared satisfied that escape was impossible, so went to stand out in the hall in front of the door. The back of his jacket was emblazoned with the words HM Prison Service.

James leaned over his mother and spoke into her ear. "Mum, Paul is here to see you. Please wake up."

After what seemed an eternity, Janice found the strength to open her eyes. "All my babies here, except poor Ben. Thank you. I love you all." Her voice was a whisper but she managed to keep her eyes open while each of them kissed her and told her they loved her. Then they fluttered closed.

Sarah was crying softly and James looked on the point of tears. Sophia wanted to cry, but the sadness she felt was more for the loss of any future relationship with her mother. The woman in the bed was a stranger to her.

Her father sat on one side of the bed with Sarah and James on the other. She and Paul stood at the end, watching their mother's breathing become more erratic. When one short, shallow breath wasn't followed by any others, Paul took her hand and squeezed it lightly. Sarah began to cry in earnest, and James held her in his arms trying to comfort her. Her father still held her mother's hand, whispering over and over that he loved her.

"I'll let the nurses know," Sophia said after a couple of minutes. "I also have a couple of calls to make so I'll be back in ten minutes or so." She so desperately needed to hear Luca's voice, it was frightening.

"I'll come with you," Paul added, his soft tone at odds with his hard man persona. "I need a smoke."

They stopped by the nurses' station and then made their way outside. Paul's guard followed behind them.

"I wanted to say sorry to you," they both began at once.

"Sorry! What do you have to apologize for?" Paul asked, surprised. "I'm the one who ruined your life."

"Oh, Paul, you didn't ruin it. You just redirected it. I want to apologize for grassing on you and then never coming to visit you in prison. I'm sorry, I was a coward." She looked up at him, wanting, needing his forgiveness.

Paul hugged her until the prison guard gruffly told him to move away. "Even without your testimony, I would still have been convicted. I left enough evidence behind. I guess maybe in a way I knew I deserved to be caught. I got in way over my head and was terrified. I didn't know where to turn. I was trying to leave the gang when Rick told me the only way out was to be dead. I was just quicker than him with the knife. Otherwise I'd have been the one lying on the pavement. Then when I turned around and saw that kid watching, I panicked. I was proud of you; you had the courage to stand up for what was right. When I heard what had happened at school, I tried to escape so I could teach those girls a lesson, but I got caught and put in solitary."

"I didn't know. But I wouldn't have wanted you to take revenge. It was horrific at the time, but it made me start a new life, and now I'm happy. I have a wonderful husband and a fabulous life in Italy."

"You're married? No one told me."

"No one knows. James only found out when he called to tell me about Mum." Her voice caught a bit. "I asked him not to say anything. I didn't want to upset her in her last hours. I'll tell Dad and Sarah tonight. Luca, my husband, will come over for the funeral. Do you think they'll let you out to attend?"

"I think so, as long as I behave myself. Of course I'll have my shadow with me." He indicated over his shoulder at the guard behind.

Paul lit the cigarette the guard passed him and took deep drags while Sophia called Luca.

"He says he'll be on the next flight out and come

straight to the flat. I guess you have to go back soon?"

"Yeah, five minutes or so. The guard's already called for the transport," Paul said.

"No matter how bleak it gets inside, Paul, I want you to know that I never stopped loving you and I never stopped being glad you were my older brother. I hope that when you get out we can go back to that relationship. I don't want to lose you, too." Sophia wiped an errant tear from her cheek and plastered on a brave smile.

"I'm not sure your husband will want you hanging out with a convicted killer."

"You're my brother. Nothing else matters."

The prison van drew up in front and the guard ushered Paul into the back. He waved at her with a wry smile before the doors slammed shut.

Her heart ached for her brother going back into incarceration. But she felt lighter than she had in weeks, knowing what she was going to do about her immediate future.

Chapter Sixteen

Luca stepped out of the cab and stared up at the decrepit brown building in front of him—Sophia's childhood home. Even if he hadn't known her troubled past, he'd still have found her former residence depressing. It couldn't have been easy for her to come back here, and now she'd lost her mother, he wanted to hold and comfort her. Tell her he loved her.

His mobile phone vibrated on his belt, but he ignored it. Chet had not been happy that he'd left everything to fly to London, saying that if he was going to put his personal life first, maybe he wasn't the man to oversee the project. Luca could lose the job. But it was nothing in comparison to the possibility of losing Sophia. In her last phone call, when she'd told him of her mother's passing, she'd sounded so distant, like she was closing all the walls around her, letting no one in.

As he strode toward the front door, a female voice called out, "Luca?"

Swiveling, he spied Olivia hurrying toward him. Although he was anxious to see Sophia as soon as possible, he couldn't be rude to her best friend, so he waited for her to reach the door.

"I thought it was you, but I wasn't sure from the back. Wow, you got here quick from Italy," she greeted him.

"I got on the first flight after Sophia called." His bag had already been packed and sitting beside his desk, waiting for her call. Waiting for her to summon him to her side where he should have been all along.

Olivia pulled a key out of her pocket and unlocked the outside door and led him toward the stairs. "You don't mind if we walk up, do you? The lifts in these buildings are disgusting."

"No, I've been sitting all day; a little exercise would be good." If he were alone he'd take the stairs two at a time, but with Olivia beside him he restrained himself and kept to her pace.

"I know it's not my place, but Sophia is my best friend…"

Was she going to tell him that Sophia needed to live her own life, have her own dream? That to make her come live with him in the little cottage would destroy her bit by bit? Olivia could save her breath, because he'd already worked that out in the two sleepless nights he'd spent alone. He couldn't watch her die a little more every day—withdraw from him until she was just a shell of herself. But neither could he live apart from her, only see her on weekends. It was the toughest decision he'd ever made, but he knew now what he was going to do. Sophia deserved to be the first to hear it.

"You know her better than anyone. I would appreciate your insight into how I can help her." At least his voice remained calm while his heart rate accelerated.

"Coming back here, her mom dying, it's been a lot harder on her than she expected. She put on a brave face for everyone, but I can tell she's crumbling inside. Don't believe her when she tells you she's fine."

It galled him to ask, but he needed to know how to reach his wife. He needed the key to unlock Sophia's heart. "Do you have any suggestions on how I can get her to open up to me? She keeps everything inside—sometimes I have no idea how she feels."

"Get her angry. I know it sounds counter-productive, but when she's angry, all the filters come off and you'll know then what she really wants."

Making his wife angry when she was dealing with the loss of her mother and lingering memories of her traumatic childhood seemed the worst idea yet. Could Olivia be trying to drive a wedge between them? Yet every time they'd had a row, it had moved their relationship forward. His parents had never argued, but he understood now that they'd had a rather sterile marriage, not one he chose to replicate. Isabella and Dante had fought a lot at the beginning of their relationship and now they had a strong bond. He wanted his marriage to reflect theirs, not his parents. And he sure as hell didn't want to become like the Wilkinses.

"Are you sure?"

She stopped on the top step and turned to him. Standing a step up, they were on eye level. "I had serious doubts about you, and this marriage, when Sophia told me. I believe now that you could be the best thing to happen to her. But you could also be the worst. I don't think she'll recover if you fail her now."

With that ominous warning, Olivia spun around and wrenched open the door to the fifth floor. He followed her silently down the narrow, dark corridor until they came to the last door. Olivia's knock was answered by a tall, fair-haired young man in his late teens.

Olivia performed the introductions while Sophia's younger brother looked him up and down. James's smile of greeting was reserved although not hostile, his handshake firm.

"Sophia, Olivia and your husband are here," James called down the corridor. He stepped back so they could enter. Soon the hallway was crowded with bodies, but all Luca cared was that at last Sophia was in his arms. He breathed deeply of her scent, burying his face in her hair, holding her tightly against him. She trembled and for a moment he thought she might cry, but then she pulled back and raised her head.

"Thank you for coming," she said, her voice weak.

"Always," he replied past a lump in his own throat.

She gave him a watery smile before glancing around. "Right, show's over. Go back to the sitting room and I'll introduce Luca to you all properly," Sophia ordered the amassed spectators.

For the next ten minutes all eyes stared at him, the mysterious husband conjured out of thin air. He offered his condolences and sipped a cup of strong tea while fielding questions about his work, his life and why they hadn't invited anyone to the wedding.

Sophia was getting tenser beside him with each question. He wanted to get her away, give her some space, time to deal with the turmoil he knew boiled just under the surface.

"*Amore*, in my haste, I forgot to pack my toothbrush. Do you think you could show me to the shop where I can purchase another?" It was a lame excuse but all he could come up with at the moment.

"Of course, let me grab my bag." She rushed out of the room as though it were on fire.

He plastered on an apologetic smile and excused himself as well, mumbling something about being back in a few minutes. Olivia gave him a conspiratorial wink as he passed.

. . .

Sophia pulled in a deep breath and rolled her shoulders, trying to relax them. Her whole body was tense, in fight or flight mode. If Luca weren't at her side, she'd jump on the Tube and just ride around and around till they kicked her off.

"Did you really forget your toothbrush?" They wandered toward the high street.

"No, I thought you needed a break from the interrogation," he replied. He took her cold hand in his warm one. Some of the warmth crept up her arm and her heart fluttered at Luca's caring.

"Then let's pop into the pub and get a drink," she said, steering him toward the local.

He held the door for her, and she inhaled deeply of his cologne as she passed by. All she wanted was to be held in his arms, sheltered from the guilt and emptiness she'd thought she'd dealt with long ago.

"What do you want?" Luca's voice near her ear sent a shiver of longing through her. Okay, maybe being held in his arms wasn't all she desired.

"Want?"

"To drink?" An answering flare of passion lit his eyes, as though he read her thoughts.

"Actually, just a ginger ale."

Luca's eyes searched hers before he stepped toward the bar. She found a quiet corner table and waited for him. The pub wasn't busy as the after dinner crowd hadn't come in yet. This was the first time she'd ever had a drink here; it was her father's hangout. A few regulars stared at her as if trying to determine if she was one of Charlie's girls, but thankfully they weren't interested enough to come over and ask.

The *clink* as Luca placed the glass on the table in front of her brought her back to the present. She could hear his phone buzz on his belt and wondered how long before he answered it. When he sat across from her rather than excuse himself to take the call, she glanced at his face. He took a sip of his red wine, put the glass down, and stared into her eyes.

"How are you?"

"I'm fine," she answered.

"No, you're not." He sat back and crossed his arms over his chest, daring her to lie to him again.

"How do you know how I feel?" This was too much—first coming back here, her mother dying, and now her husband lecturing her on how she should feel.

"I know when you're genuine and when you're putting on a front. You're pretending to be fine. I will not have you faking it with me. I am tired of your acting. If you cannot be truthful with me, then maybe it is time we put an end to this charade."

Excruciating pain filled her chest and she tried to drag in a deep breath to ease the burning. Instead all she managed was a couple of quick pants. This couldn't be happening, not today. And why was the man who hated public scenes doing this here, and now? Maybe he was too busy to wait until they got home.

"You want a divorce?" She blinked rapidly to keep the tears back; she would not cry in front of him. A look of contrition crossed his face before being replaced by a blank mask. Under the table, her right hand flew to her left, holding her rings tightly. She couldn't bear the thought of taking them off.

"I want you to stop pretending, *amore*."

Blinding fury incinerated the sense of loss and betrayal. How dare he accuse her of pretending when he was the biggest faker in this marriage? "And I want you to stop calling me *amore*, because we both know I'm not your love. Through this whole marriage I have been exactly what you wanted me to be: the elegant wife to be paraded in front of your business acquaintances, the efficient housekeeper to make sure your underwear is clean and your desk dusted regularly—"

"The enthusiastic lover?" He raised a sarcastic eyebrow. She may be faking all the rest, but that was one area of their relationship where no acting was required. He didn't need to know that.

"Yes, exactly." She took a long drink, hoping to quell the rising nausea.

"It's not enough." His harsh tone grated her heart to shreds.

"Not enough?" Several heads turned in their

direction at her raised voice. In the silence that followed, she heard his phone vibrate again. "I'll tell you what's not enough. It's not enough that I hold second place in your life, and your work is first. I'm sorry that my little family issue has pulled you out of her bed. Go on, your real love is calling, answer it!"

Luca pulled his mobile from his pocket, pressed a couple icons on the screen, and held the now silent phone out to her. Thirty-six missed calls. Forty-two unanswered emails, all with little red flags and marked URGENT.

"If this were my real love, would I be ignoring it while I sit in a pub trying to pick a fight with you?"

In a daze she handed the phone back to him. He turned the power off and returned it to his pocket, not even bothering to look at any of the messages.

"Why do you want to pick a fight with me?"

"I don't. Olivia suggested it was the only way to find out what was really going on in your heart. So, you feel second best to my work. What do you want me to do about it? Cancel the hotel contract? Because I would." He sat back again and waited for her reaction.

She was stunned. What was he saying? "You'd walk away from the hotel project if I asked? Why?"

"Because I've found something more important. Something that I love and cherish more than rebuilding Italy's past splendor. I found you. I love you, Sophia. More than I ever thought possible. You are my *amore*, and my *tesoro*, my treasure, my joy, and a million other endearments. But most important, you are my wife, my life and my reason to be."

"You love me?"

"So much it hurts to think you're not being yourself when you're with me. I feel cheated that you are holding back, saving the real you for someone else."

"I was holding back because I thought that's what you wanted. You said you didn't want a wife who loved you."

"Do you? Love me?" He held his breath.

"More than anything in the world."

That got him on his feet. He pulled her up into his arms and crushed her against him. His lips found hers, and he kissed her until she almost passed out. Dizzy from joy or lack of oxygen, she wasn't sure.

"Get a room!" someone at the bar called out.

Luca reluctantly let her go, but he kept hold of her left hand, with the other he caressed her face. "So, from here on, we agree to tell each other how we feel. Even if it is something you don't think I want to hear," he added.

She put her free hand against his heart, which thudded under her palm. "Agreed. I'll start. I feel like getting out of here and making love with you until I can't remember my own name," she replied.

"I would like nothing more. But what about your family? They're waiting for us to come back to the flat with a toothbrush," Luca reminded her.

Damn. "Alright, but I do need to stop at the chemist, because there's something I need to confirm."

"Is everything okay? You're still pale." He switched from lover to concerned husband in a heartbeat.

"I'm fine. But if my guess is right, we should probably get in some practice with Sarah's children while we're here." She expected rapturous joy to cross his face. Instead, his brow creased with concern.

"You're pregnant?"

"I think so. What's wrong? I thought you'd be happy."

"I am happy if you're happy. But what about your interior design business? I guess we could hire a nanny to care for the baby—"

"No way. After my childhood experiences, I'll look after my own children. I only started the design company now because I was bored and needed something to keep my mind off how much I love you and wanted you to love me. We'll work something out. I can wait until the time is right for us a family. Perhaps I can work part-time to begin with and see how that goes."

"I believe you can do anything you set your mind to. And I will support you every step of the way." His tender kiss left her in no doubt as to what he was feeling at that moment.

• • •

The sun warmed Sophia's back and birdsong filled the air as the family gathered around the grave. The church service had been brief, with only the family and a few friends in attendance. She swallowed a lump in her throat at the realization that her children would never meet their maternal grandmother. As if sensing her anguish, Luca leaned over and placed a gentle kiss on her temple.

She smiled up at him, and he wiped a stray tear off

her cheek. It was so liberating not to have to hide her emotions from him. If it hadn't been for her mother's passing, this would have been one of the happiest weeks of her life—showing Luca how much she loved him and basking in his returned affection. The first thing he told her every morning and the last thing every night, was how much he loved her.

Sarah's little girl, Emily, had fallen asleep on his shoulder and he shifted her into a more comfortable position. Luca was going to make a great father. He'd taken her suggestion about spending time with her nephew and nieces seriously and had passed the last four days entertaining the children while the adults sorted out the necessary arrangements for the funeral.

He'd also proved that she was more important to him than his work. He'd told his secretary to contact him only if someone was injured, that he was on compassionate leave for the rest of the week and wasn't to be disturbed. He spoke with Chet and said he would oversee the project and live on-site only if Sophia was part of the interior design team. Chet had instantly agreed and even offered her a salary in excess of the commission she would have made from the property rental firm.

When she'd told Isabella that she wasn't available to take the contract, she'd expected her new friend to be disappointed. Instead she'd also been relieved, as she'd just discovered she was pregnant as well. And with three previous miscarriages, the doctor had ordered Isabella on bed rest for at least the first four months.

Sophia had then called the chairman of the villa

rental company to tell them of their decision not to take the contract. Evidently, they had also reconsidered and decided to postpone the refurbishment of their properties for eighteen months. If she were still interested then, she would go straight to the top of their short list. It had all worked out. But none of it was as important as knowing Luca loved her.

A tiny cry drew her attention to Olivia, who was looking after Sarah's baby girl. Olivia snuggled the baby under her chin and caressed the tiny back until she quieted. Olivia's maternal instinct was so strong, Sophia could see her friend presiding happily over a gaggle of children.

Sophia was glad that Luca had convinced Olivia to come back to Italy with them. She wasn't sure if it was for her benefit, or her friend's, but she wasn't going to complain. Olivia could use a good holiday and Sophia was already planning a matchmaking opportunity to introduce her to Jonathan. It was time her friend met a real man.

If only she could do something to help her older brother. Paul stood with his hands crossed in front, his head bowed, in prayer or contrition, she wasn't sure. His guard escort stood a respectable distance away, allowing the family to grieve in private. As she'd hoped, Luca had greeted her brother with openness and ease, even offering him a job once he was released if it would help him transition back to society. In fact the prison board had said he may be eligible for early parole if he continued to be an exemplary inmate.

The minister continued his reading and Sophia

switched her attention to Sarah who was sobbing into the arms of her boyfriend. Andrew seemed to genuinely love her and Sophia was looking forward to getting to know him better when they visited later in the year. She really hoped her sister had found stability and happiness at last.

After shutting his Bible, the minister offered a few words of condolence to her father. Sarah's oldest child, little Benny, held his grandfather's hand. Silent tears coursed down her dad's face as the graveyard attendants started to shovel dirt on her mother's coffin. Hopefully, he'd be able to find some peace when he and James came to Italy as soon as her younger brother finished his coursework. With Luca's love and support, she was now looking forward to reconnecting with her family—a family that had been ripped apart by tragedy, now reunited in love.

Sophia had even managed to make peace with the specter of Kathy Summers. When her soap opera had come on the telly, Sophia had been able to watch her former nemesis without a single panicked reaction. In fact, she'd been able to dispassionately prove to herself that Kathy was truly an awful actress.

Sophia ran a hand over her still flat belly, in awe to think that a little life was growing inside her—a product of Luca's and her love. A true new beginning.

And all because the couple who hadn't wanted love had been unable to resist its power.

~~~~~~~~~~

Thank you for reading *An Inconvenient Love*. Please, please post a review where you purchased the book. Your opinion will not only help other readers decide whether to buy the book or not, it will also help me continue to write the stories that I, and hopefully you, love to read. Many promotional opportunities are only available after a book has a certain number of reviews. Please help me access these. Thank you!

Keep the story going... Catch up with Luca and Sophia and find out what happens when Jonathan and Olivia meet.

An Inconvenient Desire

When desire turns to love, it's always dangerous.

Olivia Chapman has hidden her ugly childhood scars under a glamorous modeling career and hopes she can, one day, help teenagers as desperate as she was. But first she must care for a traumatized toddler, even though that means staying with a man she has to resist. Because if there's one thing Olivia knows, it's abandonment. No way will she put her heart in the hands of a man who's sworn off commitment.

Investment banker Jonathan Davis has spent the last ten months renovating an Italian villa and getting over a nasty divorce from his supermodel wife. As a favor to a friend, he escorts Olivia to a medieval festival and battles an escalating attraction. After discovering she's a model, his self-preservation senses tell him to bail. He's never investing his heart in that stock again. But when his ex-wife abandons his previously unknown daughter at his door, it's Olivia who helps ease little Hannah's merger into his life.

Will love be strong enough to unite three lost souls into a family?

An Inconvenient Desire

Chapter One

Jonathan stared at the blinking light on his old-school answering machine. A chill swept through him despite the record-setting heat wave that currently engulfed Northern Italy. He pressed play.

"Jono, mate. When you coming back to work? Profits are down. We need you, man."

He jabbed the stop button with his middle finger, cutting off his colleague's message. He didn't want to think about going back to his career. There were almost two months left of his sabbatical before he had to return to London and the mess he'd made of his life there. Until then, he was going to enjoy his freedom and finish the renovations on his house. The newly installed swimming pool beckoned in the sweltering heat.

The workers, who were helping him find the back garden after forty years of neglect, had gone for *riposo*, the Italian version of a siesta. No one else was around. So he stripped off his clothes, ran out onto the terrace, and dove in. The frigid water knocked the breath from his body and he surfaced, gasping for air. Naked and dead of shock wasn't the way he wanted his body to be found. He was about to haul his frozen arse out of the water when the click of heels on the side patio told him he was no longer alone.

"Jonathan, are you back here?" his friend Sophia's familiar voice called out.

"Um, yeah," he replied. "But…"

Before he could ask her to wait a minute while he retrieved his clothes, Sophia and another woman rounded the corner.

"You've got quite a bit done," Sophia commented, surveying the bones of the kitchen garden that had been reclaimed from the vines that morning. "We stopped by to…" She finally looked at him and her face flamed red. Belatedly, she put her hands over her eyes.

Meanwhile, Sophia's gorgeous companion stared at him, a smile lighting her face. She put her hands on her face, too, imitating Sophia, although she left a large gap between her fingers to see through. He couldn't help laughing at her boldness.

"If you ladies would wait a moment, I'll put some clothes on."

"Yes, of course," Sophia said. "Do you want us to wait out front?"

"No need. I'll only be a second."

Sophia turned around and then nudged her friend. "Olivia," she whispered as the other woman continued to stare. He locked gazes with her and a challenge rose between them. Would she turn around or wait for the full monty?

Slowly Olivia turned her back to him and Jonathan pulled himself out of the pool. Any longer in the icy water and there wouldn't't've been much left to see. As he strode toward the house, he heard Sophia chastising her friend.

"Hey, you may be married. I'm not," Olivia replied. "Besides, he's not the first naked man I've seen. Although he does rank up there in the top ten."

Jonathan bit his tongue and stopped himself from parading back outside now that he'd warmed up a bit. He wanted to up his ranking to at least the top five spot. Instead, he pulled his clothes back on as he checked out the profile of the unknown woman through the kitchen window.

Sophia's friend was tall, with fabulous medium brown colored legs showcased by a short, black skirt and red high heels. Her dark, curly hair was piled on top of her head, with a few tendrils breaking free in spiral abandon. She had magnificent breasts and full lips and certainly ranked in the top three most beautiful women he'd ever seen—clothes on or off. As he continued to stare, she turned and caught him. Her lips curved upwards in a smile of acknowledgment.

A spark of desire lit in his lower belly, sending a rush of heat through him. Maybe he'd keep the pool water frigid if Olivia stuck around. Never taking her eyes from him, she said something to Sophia. Then she sauntered around the corner of the house. Afraid his guests would leave before he had a chance to properly meet this woman, he rushed back out onto the terrace, his bare feet burning on the hot tiles.

"Sophia, why don't you come inside out of the heat? I'll make some lemonade. Unless you'd rather have a beer?"

"A glass of water is fine. I'm sorry if we've interrupted. I just picked up Olivia from the airport and wanted to stop and invite you to come with us to the medieval festival in Brisighella tomorrow, if you don't have any plans. I should have called, but since we were driving right by…"

"No need to apologize; I'm glad you stopped. It's just so hot I thought I'd test out the new pool, but it's way too cold for a proper swim. Where's your friend?" He tried for nonchalance, but judging by Sophia's raised eyebrow, he hadn't quite achieved that level of disinterest. Grabbing the jug of water from the fridge, he poured three glasses and handed one to Sophia.

"She just popped to the car to change shoes. Before she gets back, I want to warn you that Olivia may come across as bold and confident, but she's been hurt a lot lately. Please don't play her."

He was about to reply that he had no intention of playing her friend when Olivia walked into the kitchen. His heart rate accelerated and his mouth went dry. He hadn't had an immediate reaction like that to a woman in a very long time. And judging by the way her eyes widened slightly as they met his, she felt a similar response.

"Jonathan, this is my friend Olivia Chapman. She's visiting for a couple of weeks. Olivia, this is Jonathan Davis. He's the one who rescued me when I got lost on my first day in Italy."

He shook hands with Olivia, surprised at her firm grip. "And then Sophia rescued me from bad taste," he replied. He gestured around the room. "Everything you see is a product of her design skills."

Olivia glanced around the rustic kitchen. "It's beautiful. And you have a stunning view. It must be amazing to wake up to that every morning."

Not as amazing as it would be to wake up next to you in the morning. God, he had to get a grip. Fast. He was behaving like a pubescent teenager. Not a man of thirty-one who'd already been to hell and back at the whim of a woman.

He cleared his throat. "Yes, very beautiful." His gaze locked on hers.

"So, tomorrow? Do you want to join us?" Sophia's voice broke through the fog of desire that held him captive. Even Olivia turned, as though surprised her friend was still there.

"Tomorrow?" He dragged his mind, kicking and screaming, back to the present.

Sophia laughed. "The medieval festival in Brisighella."

The voice of reason in his head told him that spending time with Olivia would wreak havoc on his newly found peace of mind. A woman on the rebound and a guy who'd sworn never to marry again—it could only end in disaster. The sensible thing to do would be to decline and spend tomorrow working on the garden.

The rest of his anatomy overruled logic.

"That sounds great. What time are you leaving?" He forced his eyes away from Olivia, who was the opposite of Sophia in coloring. Sophia had blond hair and green eyes, her pale complexion sheltered by a large brimmed hat. Olivia was dark, sultry—her mixed race parentage had blended to create a potent combination of skin tone and luscious features. But both Sophia and Olivia had the same hint of laughter in their eyes.

"Seven a.m. okay with you? Luca suggested we leave early to make the most of the day," Sophia said. Her mobile phone rang and she dug it out of her handbag. "Speak of the husband... I'll take the call on the terrace so you two can talk without having to listen to my one-sided conversation." She answered the phone as she wandered outside.

"Is this your first trip to Italy?" Jonathan asked. *Keep it simple. Keep it casual.*

"No, I've been to Rome and Milan several times. But it's the first time I've been out in the countryside and, of course, my first visit to Sophia's place."

"I'm sure you'll enjoy it. Her villa is beautiful. How long do you plan to stay?"

Her answer was preempted by Sophia's return, looking upset.

"What's wrong, Sophia? Is everything okay with Luca?" Olivia put her arm around her friend's shoulder.

"Luca's fine. It's that hotel project he's working on. There's been a hiccup with the contracts, and he needs to fly to New York right away."

"Go with him," Olivia immediately said.

"I can't, Livy. You just got here." Sophia's protests weren't as adamant as she probably hoped.

"I can hang out at your place for a few days without you. If everything you tell me is true, there's plenty to keep me busy. Go with your husband to the States—a place you've never been but have always dreamed of visiting."

"But…"

"No buts. I'll be fine."

"We were all set to go to Brisighella tomorrow," Sophia reminded her.

Olivia gave her friend an exasperated glance. "We can go when you get back."

"The festival ends this weekend."

"Then Olivia and I will go tomorrow and take lots of photos so you can see what you missed," Jonathan responded. *Why the hell did I suggest that? Has my dick learned to talk? Because obviously my brain is in my pants right now.*

"I—" Olivia began. She clearly didn't think it was a smart idea either.

"Oh, that's wonderful. If you and Jonathan are together, I won't feel so bad about leaving." The beautiful smile that crossed Sophia's face reassured him he'd done the right thing. Her interior design skills had turned his sterile renovation into a comfortable home. He owed her. And if taking her friend to a medieval festival would make her feel better, then he'd do it.

"Seven still okay for you?" he asked Olivia.

"I'll be ready," she confirmed.

"Thank you, Jonathan. I'd better get home and pack." Sophia put her water glass into the sink and turned toward the door.

"Until tomorrow," Olivia murmured as she handed him her empty glass. Their fingers touched briefly and he nearly dropped the tumbler. Her lips parted and her eyes scanned him once more before she followed her friend.

A bead of sweat slid down his spine. What had he just gotten himself into?

• • •

Early the next morning, Olivia stepped under the cool spray of the shower in one of the guest bedrooms at Sophia's villa. She was used to discomfort. Clothes that squeezed her curvy shape into the boxlike silhouette designers seemed to prefer, ridiculous shoes that pinched everywhere, and contorted positions that she had to hold for hours so a photographer could get the perfect image. It was the price she paid to be a model. A job she was damn good at. Her coping mechanism generally worked perfectly, allowing her to withstand hours of pain and still keep the smile on her face and the come-ravage-me look for which she was known in her eyes.

Her discomfort at walking into Jonathan's house yesterday, however, had all been internal. She'd reacted to him in an entirely unhealthy manner—unhealthy for her peace of mind, that was. Her body had immediately suggested all kinds of ways she could relieve the pressure that grew inside with each caress of his sky-blue eyes.

Unlike many of the male models she worked with, she was pretty sure Jonathan's muscles came from actual work, rather than hours spent in the gym. They weren't disproportionate or just for show. And when she'd caught a glimpse of his tight, white arse in the reflection from the window, she'd nearly passed out. Yes, he was one smoking hot man. What surprised her was that her immunity to pretty boys didn't seem to extend to Sophia's friend.

Maybe it was because he was more like a Norse god than a mere mortal pretty-boy. It was as though he was used to walking into a room and being instantly in charge. Jonathan's very presence was somehow powerful, disturbing; his touch almost electric. She'd had to physically force herself to move away from their contact over the water glass. His long, strong fingers could probably bring a woman to the brink of ecstasy within minutes. And his shoulder-length, light blond hair with its loose curls would give her something to hold on to as his fingers did their work. Even his blue eyes, heightened by his deep tan, could scatter her thoughts. No man had ever had that effect on her. Ever.

And that was the problem. Jonathan wasn't a man who was easily forgotten. Too bad she'd sworn off men for the foreseeable future. He would have made one hell of a swan song.

She shut off the water and toweled herself dry. The cool air slid over her body, raising goose flesh. Sophia's house was beyond magnificent. Her guest bedroom was larger than Olivia's whole flat back in London. And the gardens and postcard village on the doorstep were gorgeous. No wonder her best friend had fallen in love with Italy. And Luca.

She'd worried for Sophia when she'd entered the marriage of convenience with a man she barely knew.

Now, however, her friend not only glowed with love but also her newly discovered pregnancy. Olivia squashed a twinge of envy before it could develop into longing. Of the two of them, Sophia was suited to love and marriage and babies. Olivia, not so much. She had a career to build and didn't have time to dance attendance on any man, no matter how sexy. An image of Jonathan hauling himself out of the pool, starkers, flashed into her brain, but she repressed that as well. Although, admittedly, with a little less vehemence.

She flicked through her clothes selection. What did you wear to a medieval festival? Especially in the company of a man you were trying to keep your distance from. Burlap? She hadn't packed anything even remotely bag-like. Trousers and a loose-fitting top were as close as she could get.

The clock now showed 6:55 a.m. Damn, she was running late. Too much time in the shower fantasizing about Jonathan. She skipped the rest of her usual routine, threw a few things in the oversized handbag she'd brought for sightseeing, and headed down the stairs.

All she had to do was make it through the day with her man moratorium in place and she'd be fine. Then she caught a glimpse through the window of Jonathan arriving in a sleek sports car and the deep breath she'd taken whooshed out audibly.

Maybe she could make time for one last ill-advised affair.

Get your copy of An Inconvenient Desire now!

Thank you, Reader

I hope you enjoyed reading Luca and Sophia's story as much as I enjoyed writing it. If you did, **please, please** help others find it by leaving a **review** at your favorite retailer. Your review doesn't have to be long, but your opinion matters to me and other readers.

Want to be one of the first to know about upcoming releases, contests, and events? Sign up for my monthly newsletter at https://alexia-adams.com.

You can also chat with me on Facebook (https://www.facebook.com/AlexiaAdamsAuthor) and Twitter (@AlexiaAdamsAuth) or, of course, get in touch with me via my website (https://alexia-adams.com).

I love to hear from readers, so don't be shy.

About the Author

Alexia Adams was born in British Columbia, Canada and travelled throughout North America as a child. After high school, she spent three months in Panama before moving to Dunedin, New Zealand for a year where she studied French and Russian at Otago University.

Back in Canada, she worked building fire engines until she'd saved enough for a round-the-world ticket. She travelled throughout Australasia before settling in London—the perfect place to indulge her love of history and travel. For four years she lived and travelled throughout Europe before returning to her homeland. On the way back to Canada she stopped in Egypt, Jordan, Israel, India, Nepal, and of course, Australia and New Zealand. She lived again in Canada for one year before the lure of Europe and easy travel was too great and she returned to the UK.

Marriage and the birth of two babies later, she moved back to Canada to raise her children with her British husband. Two more children were born in Canada and her travel wings were well and truly clipped. Firmly rooted in the life of a stay-at-home mom, or trophy wife as she prefers to be called, she turned to writing to exercise her mind, travelling vicariously through her romance novels.

Her stories reflect her love of travel and feature locations as diverse as the wind-swept prairies of Canada to hot and humid cities in Asia. To discover other books written by Alexia or read her blog on inspirational destinations at https://alexia-adams.com or follow her on social media.

Other Books by Alexia:

Love in Translation series:

Thailand with the Tycoon

Will being trapped in a failing resort change more than their itinerary? When his older brother suffers a heart-attack, Caleb is sucked back into the family's virtually bankrupt business. He reluctantly travels to Thailand to evaluate a last-chance resort with the help of a translator. Getting stranded with an enchanting local was not on the agenda. Neither was falling in love.

To read an excerpt visit my website:
www.alexia-adams.com

Bali with the Billionaire

He's all business. Until she makes him her business. Ever since tragedy shattered Harrison Mackenzie's life, he's locked his passion away to focus on work. Until a captivating woman without boundaries crashes through his meticulously constructed barriers to reach the billionaire's broken heart. Is he finally ready to risk loving again?

To read an excerpt visit my website:
www.alexia-adams.com

Vintage Love series:

The Vintner and The Vixen

After witnessing a murder, Maya Tessier needs to disappear. So she escapes to the cottage in France she inherited from her great-grandmother where she hopes to start a new life and concentrate on her art. Jacques de Launay doesn't like strangers on his estate, especially when they're a sexy redhead who reminds him of all he's lost. But if he lets her stay, more than his heart may be at risk.

To read an excerpt visit my website:
www.alexia-adams.com

The Playboy and The Single Mum

Single mother Lexy Camparelli must accompany super sexy Formula 1 driver Daniel Michaud for the rest of the race season as part of her job. Will she be able to keep her life on track and her heart from crashing or will the stress of living in the spotlight bring back her eating disorder or worse, jeopardize custody of her son?

To read an excerpt visit my website:
www.alexia-adams.com

The Tycoon and The Teacher

Argentinian tycoon Santiago Alvarez will do whatever it takes to keep custody of his niece Miranda— even if it means marriage to the woman who jeopardizes his peace of mind. Genevieve Dubois is finding her way again after a traumatic experience left her unable to teach in a classroom. Helping an eight-year-old girl come to terms with the loss of her parents is challenge enough without the continual distracting presence of the sexy uncle who refuses to love. Then she discovers the real reason Santiago wants to retain guardianship of Miranda and it threatens all their futures.

To read an excerpt visit my website:
www.alexia-adams.com

The Developer and The Diva

Para siempre means forever. That's what they'd promised one another. Then she left. Now she's back, and para siempre is just two words written on the wall of the community center he's determined to tear down … and she wants to save. Will the pain of the past be too much to overcome, or will Eduardo and Anna gamble again on a love to last para siempre?

To read an excerpt visit my website:
www.alexia-adams.com

Guide to Love series:

Miss Guided

Mystery writer Marcus Sullivan is determined find someone for his younger brother Liam. Playing matchmaker on holiday in St. Lucia, Marcus tries to interest Liam in a beautiful local tour guide Crescentia St. Ives. Then Marcus gets stranded with Crescentia and the plot to match her with his brother quickly incinerates in the flames of lust. No way can Liam have her when Marcus can't keep his hands off. Too bad he can't write a happier ending to their blossoming romance.

To read an excerpt visit my website:
www.alexia-adams.com

Played by the Billionaire

Internet security billionaire, Liam Manning, made a promise to his beloved brother, Marcus, to complete his mystery-romance manuscript. Problem is that Liam's experience with women is limited to the cold-hearted supermodels he usually dates. So falling back on his hacking skills, he infiltrates an online dating site to find a suitable woman to teach him about romance—regular guy style. What he didn't expect was for the feelings to be so … real. Can Liam finish the novel before Lorelei discovers his deceptions and, more critically, before she breaches the firewall around his heart?

To read an excerpt visit my website:
www.alexia-adams.com

His Billion-Dollar Dilemma

Simon Lamont is an ice-cold corporate pirate. But when he arrives in San Francisco to acquire a floundering company and is accosted by a cute engineer with fire in her eyes, it takes all Simon has to maintain his legendary cool. Helen will do whatever it takes to change his mind, and if that means becoming the sexy woman Simon didn't know he wanted, so be it. If only she wasn't about to walk into her own trap...

To read an excerpt visit my website:
www.alexia-adams.com

Alexia Adams

Masquerading with the Billionaire

World-renowned jewelry designer Remington Wolfe is competing for the commission of a lifetime and someone is trying to destroy his company from the inside. He's in for more than one surprise when his unexpected rescuer turns out to be a sexy computer specialist with a sharp tongue and even sharper mind.

To read an excerpt visit my website:
www.alexia-adams.com

Romance and Intrigue in the Greek Islands:

The Greek's Stowaway Bride

Hoping to make it to North Africa to free her uncle, Egyptian heiress Rania Ghalli stows away on the yacht of Greek millionaire Demetri Christodoulou. But when Egyptian agents board the boat, she can either jump overboard … or claim she's Demetri's new bride. Demetri needs a wife to complete a land purchase so he agrees to play along—if she'll agree to a real marriage. But keeping the vivacious heiress out of his heart will be a lot harder than keeping her on his ship…

To read an excerpt visit my website:
www.alexia-adams.com

Romance in the Canadian Prairie:

Her Faux Fiancé

Take one fake engagement to a man she once loved, stir in a very real pregnancy, add a marriage of convenience, bake in the heat of revenge and you get the mess that has become Analise's life.

To read an excerpt visit my website:
www.alexia-adams.com

Business Trip Romance

Singapore Fling

Lalita Evans's father hired Jeremy Lakewood in the family's international conglomerate, and now he's tagging along as she oversees their interests across eight countries in three weeks. Will Jeremy risk his livelihood and all the success he's achieved to win the woman who haunts his dreams?

To read an excerpt visit my website:
www.alexia-adams.com

Daring to Love Again Series:

The Sicilian's Forgotten Wife

Bella Vanni has accepted that her presumed-dead husband is long gone, so it's a huge shock when he knocks on her door and announces his desire to resume their marriage. She can't trust his answers on where he's been or why he left, and she certainly isn't keen to walk away from the life she's constructed for herself in his absence. But when Matteo's freedom is threatened, Bella must decide which is most important to her: everything she's painstakingly built or a second chance

at a love that never died.
To read an excerpt visit my website:
www.alexia-adams.com

Manufactured by Amazon.ca
Bolton, ON

29319461R00131